A House Out of Time

Also, by Bruce Macfarlane

Science Fiction
Out of Time
A Drift Out of Time
A House Out of Time
The Space Between Time
The Time Palace of Mars

The Time Travel Diaries Trilogy

Short Stories
The Webs of Time

The Butterfly Effect
An Audio script for the Time Travel Diaries

History
Notes on Arthurian Literature

A House Out of Time

The third book from
The Time Travel Diaries of
James Urquhart and Elizabeth Bicester

by
Bruce Macfarlane

2nd Edition

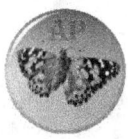

Aldwick Publishing

Copyright © 2018 Bruce Macfarlane
Aldwick Publishing
www.aldwickpublishing.com
All rights reserved.

ISBN-978-1-9164024-3-0

:

Dedication

To my Wife Julia

A House Out of Time

Preface

Here is the third book from the Time Travel Diaries of James Urquhart, science lecturer and occasional rambler, living in 2015 and Elizabeth Bicester, Victorian Cambridge graduate, whom he met at a cricket match in 1873.

They are narrated by Professor Rolleston who discovered the diaries and spent his life, when not hunting fairies, trying to understand their contents and the reasons for their existence.

--~--

www.timetraveldiaries.co.uk

A House Out of Time

Acknowledgements

Images & Illustrations.
Art work and photographs by author using digital manipulation PicsArt for Android and PaintShop Pro.

Book Cover:
Author's own photo of sunset with PicsArt

Chapter 2 The house out of time -Old House, Cornwall.
Chapter 4 Time capsule – Sculpture and Gordale Scar, Yorkshire.
Chapter 7 "The Edge of Time"
Chapter 9 Depiction of Martian. Gargoyle – Wells Cathedral.
Chapter 10 Sculpture West Dean plus Author's own sunrise photo.
Chapter 11 Martian spaceship plus Moon.
Chapter 12 Visigoth Church, Asturias.
Chapter 14 North York Moors and carriage.

A House Out of Time

Contents

A House Out of Time

Introduction

James and Elizabeth have "retired' to a life of ease in a new time world in 2016 after helping the Martians save the Earth and their own planet.

Unfortunately, Elizabeth thought it would be a good idea to visit her ancestral home at Hamgreen to see what had become of it.

….Such is the curiosity of women.

You see, although Elizabeth's house is always there, you can't find it on a map.

Yet, it's been there since before the Great Comet arrived and usually there's a Martian sitting on the gate post.

The trouble is time inside the house is often different to that outside. It depends on which door you go through.

You really have to make sure you are wearing the right clothes when you pay a visit.

$--- \sim ---$

A House Out of Time

Chapter One

E

This new world which James and I share is a delight. He is back in his beloved college and I have a pleasurable occupation lecturing on, and helping to design, Victorian fashions.

Although there are many great upheavals in the world as we try to save our planets, everyone appears to be united in the belief that we have only two precious worlds and to survive we must look after them and each other. I sincerely hope we are in a time line where we can make it. The fact that the Martians are here with their ability to glimpse into the future gives me faith in this.

However, despite the comforts we enjoyed I found myself often drawn by the proximity of my home at Hamgreen to pay a visit and find out who resided there. Perhaps I had mentioned this too often to James using what he calls, rather unfairly, persistent repetition, for this morning just after breakfast he surprised me by offering to take me there. I agreed immediately.

"There's just one thing, though," he said, "I've been thinking about it as well and I've just spent a bit of time looking it up."

I had noticed while we were waiting for the tea to brew James had been studiously playing with his phone with a puzzled expression upon his face but I had presumed that, as usual, he was absorbed in understanding a new scientific wonder. Such studies would often keep him amused for an hour or so and were accompanied by much scribbling and mutterings followed by an excited presentation of his conclusions to which I always tried to convey a visage of considerable interest and understanding. On this occasion there was no need to affect such an expression. I ran over to him to examine his phone.

"What does it say?" For I wished to know what happened to my family.

"Nothing. It has no history. In fact, it's not even there!"

I did not understand. "Is there nothing? Not even a map or picture?"

"No."

"So in this world my home does not exist?"

"I didn't say that."

I looked into his eyes. I could see he was thinking the same as me. A distraction of a visit had become a necessity.

I came close and whispered, "Shall I pack the 'full gear' as you call it?"

"Yes, and don't forget those red stockings," he said putting his arm around my waist. I responded as expected.

"Why? Do you wish to wear them, James? I do not think you will look very fetching."

We quickly collected, or should I say I packed, what we needed including a selection of late Victorian clothes in case we entered my world again. James diplomatically decided to leave this to me and went for his carriage as he had come to realise through a number of rather embarrassing experiences that on the question of Victorian fashion I had an advantage.

He had bought a new leaf green, electric vehicle containing four red upholstered seats which he had purchased for a song at a railway auction. He thought they would remind me of my own time and indeed I found their comfort on long journeys did make me wish for a modern seat designed by someone who had some understanding of a lady's posture. It was also fitted with a large luggage space at the rear which James said he thought, rather cheekily I must say, was sufficient even for my expectations. I have often wondered how lightly men travel but I have come to realise it is only possible if they have some dependence on another such as a dutiful lady companion to provide any items which they had not thought necessary on departure.

Once James had loaded the car and managed to close the lid with a little effort after removing the luggage twice and repacking it, we made ourselves as comfortable as possible in the carriage and fitted the harnesses. James examined the guidance system. In this world vehicles drove themselves and a manual operation was only required if a destination was not available.

"That's weird. Hamgreen doesn't exist on the GPS." he said, "Oh dear, I'll have to drive it myself."

He had the look of small boy with a new toy.

After various near shaves accompanied by minor expletives by James on the skills of other road users and a rather unfair remark on my map reading at one point, not to mention the horn blowing from passing carriages we arrived a little dishevelled at Hamgreen late in the afternoon.

My suggestion that as the guidance system contained our home address and therefore would not require manual intervention on our return was met with a little disappointment by James though he cheered up on my reminding him of his dexterity in avoiding a bus and wagon coming towards us on what turned out to be a one-way street.

---~---

3

J.

I must admit my driving was a little rusty though Elizabeth was good enough not to comment too much. However, on two rather hairy occasions she did grab my arm rather tightly. She also appeared to have her eyes closed on much of the journey. This I'm sure led to the small altercation just outside Chichester on map reading and my misunderstanding of the directions 'left' and 'my other left'. The later apparently is Victorian for "turn right" and should be obvious to anyone with a modicum of sense.

--- ~ ---

E.

We arrived at my home a little after three o'clock in the afternoon. A hundred years had passed since I'd last seen it and I felt a certain sense of foreboding for out of the corner of my eye as we turned off the road I saw, perched upon the remaining stone gate pillar, one of the familiar small, winged creatures. James saw it too and we had a whispered conversation about its portent. But when I looked again it had vanished. They always seemed to be with us, like guardians, although if they were, I did not understand their purpose.

We passed through the gate and drove slowly on to the gravelled courtyard. As we alighted from James' carriage the sun momentarily hid behind a cloud and my flesh felt a dampness in the warm summer air causing me to pull my shawl tightly across my shoulders. As I stood there I saw the old Lodge with the eyes of my childhood and absorbed its familiarity but then my maturity espied a certain neglect. It needed a coat of paint on the windows, a lime wash on the

ashlar facade, and the gutters cleared of weeds, yet around
the porch there was evidence of someone caring for the
flowers.

$$--- \sim ---$$

J.

The Martian was sitting almost motionlessly on the gate
pillar. I had learnt to watch them out of the corner of my
eye for if they saw you looking at them directly they often
vanished. This one seemed to be gazing intently towards the
lodge. I could see its wings, if that's what they were, gently
fluttering or shimmering. But as I turned to Elizabeth and
pointed towards it, the creature faded from view.

*What's it doing here?" she whispered.

"I don't know. We've not seen them near us since
Newgrange. I wouldn't be surprised if we're heading for
another time split."

"Then we must stay close to each other. But be careful as
we cross the gate, James. It may be a portal."

This brought me to my senses. I drove the car through
the gate slowly, Elizabeth holding my arm. I felt no change.
I looked behind and was reassured to see a car drive past
the entrance along the road. We continued up the tree lined
drive over a carpet of dying autumn red and orange leaves.
It was enchantment itself but before I knew it we emerged
into the gravelled court yard of the Lodge. I looked around.
Everything seemed normal. Just another old dilapidated
Georgian house buried in the woods of Sussex.

I parked the car in the centre of the courtyard and got out.
Elizabeth took my hand and we walked towards the
entrance. Although I'd visited Elizabeth's house many times

it was the first time I had really looked at its style and structure. The main porch was guarded by two Georgian pillars with very worn copies of Roman capitals almost hidden by the leaves of the Virginia creeper which had taken over much of the front wall. But the door frame, instead of fitting in with the eighteenth-century fashion, was rounded in the Romanesque style. The studded wooden door was distinctly Medieval. At the bottom of the left pillar was a rather worn oval recess about six inches deep and underneath were some scratch marks which looked vaguely like letters. I said, "Do you know what this is?"

"No. I have always presumed a piece had been broken, perhaps by a carriage."

I bent down to have a look at the markings. I thought I could just make out V, Q or O and T. I drew her attention to it. She looked perplexed.

"Mmh. That is strange. I had not noticed that before. Maybe the servants or perhaps the scribblings of an ancestral child."

$$--- \sim ---$$

E

On the approach to the door I sought and held James' hand for we were too aware that this place had been a time node and my fear of separation at such places always welled up in me. I sensed the same in James by the tightness of his grasp. The markings James had found were a mystery for I had lived here for most of my life and I am sure I would have noticed them. But as we stood up and mounted the stone steps to the door I heard the sound of bolts being withdrawn and the turning of keys. I held my breath waiting to see who resided in my home. The door slowly opened and revealed a blank grey translucent wall! I let out a small cry for first a hand then a lady's dress appeared through the dark surface and then, there was my sister Flory standing in the porch. She did not look a day older than when I had left her after our visit to our father in 1873.

---~---

Chapter Two

E.

We stood before my sister Flory in the courtyard. At first, I thought I saw fear in her eyes but it was merely the shock of recognition. "Oh, it is you, Elizabeth! Where is Father? Is he not with you?"

This was unexpected. We said we had not seen him since we last visited.

"So if you have not met him what brought you here?"

It was sometime since our last visit to my home. I could not recall the date, but I remember it was full summer in 1873. I surmised therefore, that if we had arrived back in the same year, for Flory it was at least two months since we had last met. I held that thought and said, "It was a whim, Flory. I just wanted to see our home again."

I noticed her eyes were glancing up and down the drive. I wondered what she was looking for.

I said, "What is the matter, Flory? What can you see?"

"It is so different out here. The autumn colours have changed, and it so warm as if summer has returned."

I heard James exclaim under his breath and squeeze my hand sharply. I realised a time portal was located within the doorway.

Flory, sensing our concern, came close to me and regarding our clothes whispered, "Have you come from the future?"

I said, "Yes and no. I cannot explain it but we believe we are in the future. We did not expect to find you here. We only wanted to find out what happened to you and our home."

This I could see perplexed her for a moment then her eyes widened. "Oh, now I understand what has happened. This door has become a portal across time. You must come in quickly, both of you. I am not myself out here but be warned, inside it is early winter. Henry has the fire on in the drawing room."

We entered the hall. It was exactly as I had left it when we said goodbye to my father, but the temperature had dropped alarmingly! Between outside and here there was evidently a time slip! I turned to the door and saw it shimmer and as she closed it I thought I glimpsed an autumn scene.

"Flory, what has happened? And what year is it here?"

Her words came tumbling out mixed with the emotion of fear.

"It is 1873. We were in our own world until a month ago then one morning I went out to the gate as usual with Lilly to collect the milk. The weather was unaccountably hot for late autumn. When we reached the gate there was no milk churn. Lilly said she would go up to the farm but just as we approached the road we were nearly run over by one of those contraptions of James!"

"Did it stop?" said James.

"We did not wait to find out. We ran as fast as we could back into the Lodge and told Henry. He did not believe us at first and went to see for himself. He quickly came back confirming what we had seen."

"What did you do? It must have been frightening."

"Yes, it was! Henry, poor brave man, decided to ride to the next village. I was not keen on this and wished to go with him but he refused my offer and said I must stay. However, I got him to agree to take Smethers and suggested they take the green road as from my experience in your time the carriages of James' world are rarely seen there."

I understood. I remembered due to another unaccountable error in map reading, for whom the responsibility has still not been quite resolved in one party's view, James and I found ourselves in such a lane after what should have been a simple excursion to Stoughton. The farmer was very obliging with his tractor in rescuing us and so was James the next day in Chichester with a purchase of a new pair of evening shoes.

But to return to the subject. I asked Flory what had she discovered.

"Oh dear. I can hardly bring myself to tell you. They came across a group of strangely clad people with knapsacks who told them to give way. Henry was furious. He ordered them to get off his land and then chased half a dozen of them across a field. He then proceeded to the Farm, except..."

Flory had stopped speaking and covered her lips with her hand. I encouraged her to continue.

"Very well. But please believe us. He found the farm was not there! Just the ruins of the cow shed. This, he admitted, unnerved him and fearing for my safety returned to the Lodge."

James said, "He shouldn't feel too bad. Faced with that I would have legged it as well."

"But that is not all!" said Flory, "That evening there was a loud knock at the door. We both opened it. At first, we saw nothing then Henry went for his gun and as we crossed the threshold, we saw a strange carriage with a flashing blue light and a strangely uniformed man and a woman in trousers! They claimed they were police constables, and they looked very nervous."

"I'm not surprised," said James, "Seeing you two

materialise through a blank wall must have frightened the hell out of them."

"Be that as it may. They reprimanded us severely for chasing people across a field. I can tell you it took some effort to dissuade Henry from using his shotgun and to persuade him to offer an abject apology. But enough. Please come and see him. He is out of his time and at a loss. And Elizabeth, please cover yourself."

--- ~ ---

J.

Having visited many old Georgian National Trust houses put back into the style of their origins I'd forgotten how much the Victorians had changed them. Gone was that airy Jane Austen look. Instead every space seemed to be utilised. There was hardly a place on the heavy, dark wooden, sideboards which wasn't cluttered with porcelain, and upturned glass jars of dead flowers and animals. The large round table in the centre with its massive lion feet was draped in a cover which I'm sure was thicker than my carpet at home and was covered in books, paper and pens. Between the dark crimsoned, peacock patterned, curtains a soft light came through the window which had just enough strength to give some illumination to most of the room. In the far corner below what looked like a number of ancestral portraits, all of which suggested that eating game pie was the only meal of choice, I noticed the obligatory upright piano. Except this one was covered in sheets of music suggesting at least someone in the house took an interest in it. The main feature though was the distinctly un-Victorian fireplace which would have found a welcome home in a castle keep.

I remembered one windy winter night its ability to blow hot embers onto the blackened hearth rug and direct the heat anywhere but into the room had occupied much of the conversation.

Henry was sitting in a dark red upholstered wing chair, dressed in his hunting gear with a shotgun and club by his side, giving the impression he hadn't been listening to the conversation about his 'dastardly cowardice'. He always gave me the impression of the kind of Victorian gentleman who regarded not being willing to stand in a line dressed in non-camouflage red in order to catch cannonballs as a weakness of character. How he was dealing with this situation which involved him running away without a shot being fired I don't know. But as I approached him with some trepidation, remembering our first meeting at that cricket match, he suddenly looked up at me and leapt out of his seat. Before I could run and hide, and NOT behind Elizabeth's skirts as was later suggested by someone, he grasped me with both hands and said,

"Thank God you are here, Mr Urquhart. You are my only hope. What is that world out there?"

Before I could think of a reply he noticed Elizabeth.

"Forgive me, Elizabeth. Where are my manners? How are you? Are you ...."

He had noticed her short skirt and blouse.

"Are you not a little cold?"

Thank God she wasn't wearing jeans.

Elizabeth immediately adopted the time and occasion.

"Please forgive me for my clothes. I did not expect to be in this time otherwise I would have dressed for the occasion."

"It is of no consequence save to reinforce the reality we

have perceived. But please, once again, my manners. Sit down; may I bring you tea?"

Ah! Victorian tea time. Almost as good as my Aunts used to treat me to in Scotland as a child. Having scoffed two pieces of shortbread and a large slice of sponge cake I said. "So how have you survived the last month?"

"It is simple, Mr Urquhart. We have found by experiment that if we leave via the veranda we are in our world. If we try to leave by the front entrance, we enter yours."

"What about the servants? Do they know?"

"No. We have prohibited them from leaving or entering via the front. We have bolted and locked the door and only Flory and I have the keys."

Elizabeth turned to me and said, "What if this is only temporary and we are trapped back here in time?"

I immediately got up and went the window. My car and more importantly our luggage had vanished!

I turned to Henry and said, "Excuse me, but can I look out of the front door? I need to see if the future is still there."

He looked at Flory and nodded. I accompanied her to the door and after she had unlocked it I looked out. Nothing just blankness. Then without thinking I stepped out onto the porch. There was a slight shimmer in the air and my car appeared. The brief moment of relief vanished almost immediately when I looked back and saw just a grey wall in the open door. I literally flew back through the portal into the house. Elizabeth was standing there. She was really angry.

"You absolute fool! What did you think you were doing? I could have lost you!"

And she stormed off into the study. I quickly followed.

She stood by the mantelpiece, shaking. I went to her and she saw my look and melted in my arms.

"Oh, James! You idiot. We must learn to think before we act. But as we have now established both worlds exist in juxtaposition we must somehow capitalise on it."

"So what do we do? Go to the future and look for your father while it still exists or stay here?"

$$--- \sim ---$$

E.

I could not leave my sister and cousin in this state of limbo for I would not forgive myself if anything untoward happened. What would become of them? They did not exist in my new world. But then I remembered my father. I turned to Flory and said, "Do you know where father is?"

She hesitated then after looking at Henry for consent said, "I'm sorry, Elizabeth. I could not bring myself to tell you. But on the first day of this phenomenon, he left by the front door with the intention of finding you. He guessed that out there was James's world and he was going to travel to Chichester to find you. He has not returned."

"Did you not try to stop him?"

"Of course I did. But I was on my own and as you know when Father is determined, well, it is difficult."

I did not blame Flory. This was a cruel fate. My family was split between two worlds. I turned to James for support.

After a rather long moment in which he eventually realised we were all looking at him for help he said, "If we stay here we need to get our clothes from the car."

I was hoping for a little more guidance and gently parked his suggestion. "No, James. We have clothes here. We must not be in haste though I fear haste might be all we have if this disparity in time is temporary."

He thought a bit more while we waited for enlightenment though not without sympathy. Poor James. Here he was in my world with three Victorians expecting him to solve our problems. I could not imagine it the other way around.

Then he said with what looked like relief on his face at finding a solution. "OK. This is it. We have to find your father. Why? Because he may have learnt something about this time shift. And also, if he is dressed in his usual fashion he's going to stick out like a sore thumb."

My father's 'usual' fashion was not eccentric but I agreed he would be taken for one very quickly if anyone engaged with him in conversation.

"But," said Henry, "Why has he not returned?"

"I've no idea but it's possible because he can't or he's lost." said James.

The second I had considered but not the first. What could prevent him from returning?

James continued. "Look. As far as I can see there is nothing to be gained by staying here. Everyone's in stasis. We can't go looking for him here because it's 1873. We need to go to the future."

"But he may return while we are away," said Flory.

"In that case," James replied, "you will be here to look after him and if we don't find him we'll return here."

I could see he was right. I discussed this with Flory and after some sisterly words verging on argument she acquiesced, "You are right, Elizabeth. We still have our own world here, even though we can only find it by the rear of the house. We will wait for you, but please be quick."

Henry was in agreement. "Do not worry yourselves. I will

be here to protect Flory. It is Old Bicester who needs help."

--- ~ ---

Chapter Three

J.

We drove back to Chichester using the guidance system. I did offer to drive but Elizabeth thought after the 'adventure', as she called it, I might not be as sharp as required. Sometimes it is a good idea to be reminded of your limitations.

The trees were in full autumn colour across the Downs. I remarked, "Autumn seems to arrive quickly in this world, Elizabeth."

"Yes, the seasons do progress at a pace. No doubt the heat aids it so."

The increase in carbon dioxide which was now at last under some control had caused an incredible regrowth in vegetation throughout the world. But unfortunately it had also brought a deluge of rain, and most crops that depended on months of sunshine such as wheat and barley had disappeared to be supplanted by rice.

When we arrived at our house we found a pile of letters on the floor.

"God. The postman seems to have emptied his sack through the door." I said with some surprise. As I picked up the pile Elizabeth noticed the puzzlement in my face.

"Are you well? You look perplexed."

I looked at my phone. Just as I suspected. We had moved a week forward in time.

I said, "That time portal at your home has lost us a week."

But Elizabeth wasn't listening. She had noticed a particular handwritten letter in the pile. She picked it up and examined it.

"I think this is from my father!"

She quickly opened it and read the contents.

"He is here, James! What is the date today?"

"20th of October."

"This was written yesterday."

"Where is he?"

"He is in Midhurst. I have an address. He is staying with a Mr. Horace Hyatt. Oh, and he apologises for eating our food and also taking one of your suits."

"I've only got one suit!"

"Really, James? It is a wonder I am seen out with you. We must buy you more before I am commented on," she said with that impish smile of hers. I replied in fashion.

"And where shall we put them? For some reason my wardrobe is full."

"I could not let all that space go to waste. Besides I presumed you had another wardrobe as I thought those that I found were just remnants for gardening."

She had now put on that demure expression of hers which she used when indulging in a bit of banter.

I looked at my clothes and then at Elizabeth's and agreed perhaps a little effort was required on my part. I must have looked a little dejected at this point because she came over and kissed me. I returned it. After a short while I said,

"Anyway, who is this Mr Hyatt?

"Let me have your phone, James."

I reluctantly gave it to her. My sister, Jill, had commented once that taking my phone from me was like Gandalf trying to get the Ring from Bilbo. Rubbish. It's just a rather delicate instrument which needs looking after.

"Do I type the name in here?" she said.

I looked. "Yep. Then press that button there. That's it."

And with a few seconds my dearest Victorian was surfing the net like a pro.

"Ah, I have found only one but he was Headmaster to Mr. H. G. Wells!"

"That's our man. What's he doing here? Let's have a look."

"Give me a moment, James." I withdrew my hand which had nearly had my phone in my grasp. "Ah yes. He has been at this address not five weeks."

"How did you get that?"

"It is simplicity itself. You just ask the right question. And I thought it needed a wizard to operate it."

And she looked at me with mock disappointment.

"No, Elizabeth. It's designed for idiots with no knowledge of how it works."

"Gosh, until now I had not realised what little mental capacity was needed to live in your world. But now, come to think on it, it would explain a lot of our actions."

Before I could reply she said, "Oh look, this one shows the weather. And oh! this one must be your camera. Let me take a picture of you."

And she turned it to me, "Is it this button? Oh yes! There you are. I have a picture of you at last."

She showed me the image. "Can you print this for me as a keepsake?"

Her voice sounded weak. I looked at her. A tear had formed in her eye. I had forgotten how fragile our existence was together. I turned on the printer and made her four small copies. "And now I wish something from you," I said.

"What do I have that you need? Surely not my red stockings again?"

"If you mention those once more you'll find you'll be needing a new pair soon after."

"Not too soon after I hope, James," she said with an inviting smile that took not a little resisting.

What a girl.

I then gave her a pair of scissors. She understood and cut me a small lock of her hair. I inserted it in a small envelope and put it in my wallet.

"Now," I said, "what about your father?"

--- ~ ---

E.

I carefully put three of James' pictures in separate bags and the fourth within a secret pocket about my person. Then I said, "We must go to Midhurst."

"Yes, but we should wait until tomorrow. It's getting dark."

"No, I cannot wait. My father is out there and time might change again before we know it."

Despite my protestations I eventually and reluctantly agreed to his proposal to wait until the morrow on the condition that he cook an Italian pasta dish for in truth I was rather hungry after our adventure.

To my dismay we arose later than expected. Never-the-less, James insisted we should partake in what he describes as one of his heart stopping breakfast 'fry ups' before leaving as we had no idea when we might get another meal. I then quickly packed while James cleaned the dishes and then we drove up to Midhurst. Luckily the address was in James's guidance machine and thus thankfully the journey was uneventful. Mr Hyatt was staying in rooms close to the old chemist's shop on Church Road. He greeted us wearing a dark suit jacket and light grey trousers. He was quite small and rather rotund. His face, on which grew white sideburns and a heavy moustache, had a cheerful complexion. I noticed a number of buttons were undone on his green waistcoat which judging by his girth had not been fastened for some time and suggested he enjoyed fine food. That familiar aroma of tobacco which I had come to associate with my time surrounded him. When we introduced ourselves he invited us in immediately and there in the sitting room was my father. He was still wearing James's suit. I ran to him and hugged him.

"Ah, you received my letter. I was not quite sure how the postal service operates in your world but your presence indicates it works well."

"Yes, I received your letter and came post haste." Carefully omitting the delay of a night. "But what are you doing here, Father?"

"And," said James, "more importantly, how did you get here?"

"It is an interesting story. Please sit down." said my father, indicating the retelling might take some time. "He motioned us to an old sofa. "Good. Now, first of all I went to your home in Chichester."

"How?" said James, "It's over 10 miles!"

"I must admit I did not have a plan but as I walked down the road a carriage stopped and the driver asked me if I was well."

"I suppose your clothing must have fascinated him," said James.

"That is exactly what he said. He wanted to know where I bought my clothing as next week, he was attending a party in which my fashion would be perfect for the occasion. I was not sure whether to take this as a compliment.

However, this gave me the opportunity to embellish a story which might assist me."

"Father, you didn't take advantage of the man?"

"Heaven forbids, Lizzy!"

I turned to James and said, "I expect you have noticed my father can spin a story into any web of his choosing."

"I couldn't possibly comment, Lizzy," James grinned, using my family nickname of which he knew I did not approve.

My father noticed as well but continued, "I told him I was attending a similar function in Chichester that evening but my daughter had taken my carriage again."

"You made me an accomplice to your story!" I exclaimed.

So having compromised my position, honour and respectability I am now incorporated into a legend in which I did not participate! There will be nothing left of my reputation in my old age.

"Well, you must admit, Lizzy," he said "there is some truth in what I said about your borrowings. I remember that time when you were infatuated with that young man at Horsham and you…"

I interrupted him quickly. "Please continue with your story, Father."

Luckily, he continued. But not before I noticed by the expression on James' face that he was filing 'Horsham' away for future use.

"Anyway, on hearing my story he immediately offered to take me in his carriage on condition I told him all about what I knew about Victorian manners and etiquette. I must say it was an exciting ride and the comfort first class."

"And the poor chap has gone away with all the knowledge and fashions of the 1850s," I said.

"What's wrong with that?" said James.

"Would you go out in the clothes of your father or grandfather?"

"Point taken, Lizzy."

"James! Don't use that name."

"Sorry," he said, still grinning,

I had discovered that when James and Father were together the constraints of convention were somewhat loosened, and they were likely to edge each other on. This was especially noticeable in the presence of what I would call 'respectable' company.

"So, Lizzy, if you will let me finish my story. When I arrived at your abode, I thought I had the wrong place as it was much smaller than I expected."

He looked at me with air of a kind father whose daughter had not quite come up to his expectations. I thought best not to pursue this and thankfully nor did he. "There was no answer, so I tried the door, and it opened."

James and I looked at each other. We were sure we had locked up before leaving.

"I could immediately see it was comfortable and homely and knew it was your house because I recognised one of your green dresses laid over a chair. There was also a pile of ironing on the table and plates unfinished in the kitchen. I presume your maid had taken advantage of your absence and left without completing her duties."

"We do not have one, Father." I could see he had difficulty with that. "We live alone, Father, and we share the household duties."

He looked at James with some surprise. "Do you mean you share all housework without help?"

James said, "Well actually, Elizabeth does the bathroom

and toilet. Apparently, I don't quite come up to her expectations in those areas."

"And I'm sure nor would I. This is rather Bohemian. But by the bye. I took the liberty of searching for clues for your whereabouts but found nothing. Just then your sister Miss Urquhart arrived."

"You saw Jill?" said James.

"Yes. She had been upstairs. We rather shocked each other. I must say she was rather scantily dressed even for the weather. When I said I was Lizzy's father she immediately sought to take care of me. Fed me a most delicious pie and suggested I should borrow James' clothes. I hope you do not mind?"

"My sister gave you my last Turners pie?" exclaimed James. He looked dejected.

"I'm sorry, James, I did not know. I can tell you it did not go to waste. She also said that you would not miss your suit as she thought you used it only for gardening purposes.

"Anyway, I remembered you had told me about Mr Wells and I thought perhaps he might be at home in your time and you were with him. Your sister, who thankfully had some understanding of your adventures thought this was worth exploring too and offered to take me there. I can tell you I have never had such an extraordinary and exciting journey and I can tell you I have experienced the Roaring Forties. Such speed and your sister drove which such skill and determination that I am sure she would give Lizzy a run for her money in a dog cart race."

"Don't count on it," retorted James, "I've been in two dog carts with your daughter and I'm sure she'd beat my sister hands down."

"I might take you up on that wager. It would be a singular

entertainment as I have noticed that when women are in competition with each other they do it in some earnest. But to continue. When we arrived at Midhurst, we went to the chemist shop where I believe Mr Wells had worked and asked if they knew him. I had not realised how famous he was. However, the shop assistant told me he was long dead. I was just about to leave when the shop manager who had been listening to my conversation mentioned that he had let a room to a Mr Hyatt not five weeks since who had asked the same question. I immediately asked if I could meet him and he was good enough to bring me here. Oh, by the bye, before the manager left he said that if I was looking for work in horticulture, he would point me in the right direction."

He was now smiling at James who in return was wagging a finger at him with a similar humorous countenance conveying the impression that the fund of gardening jokes about his only suit had been exhausted.

I then asked what had happened to Jill.

"Once she saw I was safely ensconced with a kindred spirit she said she would go back to Chichester in case you turned up there. She gave me a telephone number to dial if I required any assistance. There is a telephone here as you can see but despite our best efforts neither Mr Hyatt or I have been able to understand its function to communicate with anyone."

---~---

J.

While wondering how many more jokes about my clothes were going to be dug out, I noticed Mr Hyatt was keeping very quiet in his chair, listening and fiddling with a pipe. It was time to fit this man into the jigsaw so I turned to him and said, "Mr. Hyatt, we would like to thank you very much for looking after Elizabeth's father but would you mind telling us how you got here and why?"

"Not at all, Mr Urquhart. Your friend Mr Wells arranged it."

Ah! Mr Wells. I was still not sure whether he was a friend or just helping us to suit his own purposes but I kept that to myself.

"And how?" I said feeling yet another time story coming.

"I do not understand everything. As you may be aware, Herbert was a bright pupil at my school in Midhurst. What you may not be aware of is I had met him before when he was much older."

"Pardon?" I said waking up suddenly.

"Yes, it is a conundrum with which I am still having difficulty. He said that shortly I would meet him as a pupil and he wished to ensure that his younger self was given a grounding in modern scientific knowledge. You can imagine I thought this was some prank by a madman. But he persuaded me to come to his carriage where he presented me with a number of scientific books. They were beautifully written with many coloured photographs and graphs. I had never seen the likes. But what shocked me were the dates of publication. They were all written in the early twentieth century! I swear it. There were books on time and space, anthropology, chemistry and the transmutation of the elements. He insisted that I should read these before he came as a pupil and that I should impart as much of this knowledge as I could into his brain. He seemed to regard the concept that the fourth dimension was a time quantity rather than a spatial one as especially important. Apparently, he was of the belief that one could travel through time!"

Only just having met this bloke for the first time I felt a little test of his veracity was required. If that's the right word.

"So what did you think of Einstein's theory of relativity?"

"I found, Mr Urquhart, that the mathematics were beyond me, though a book by a Mr Feynman helped me enormously to understand the concepts."

Ah, Richard Feynman, I thought. How would have I got through college without him. I also thought it best, as Mr Hyatt had been headmaster to a boys only school, not to tell him that Elizabeth had cracked Einstein's relativistic tensor calculus in one evening. Though I must admit it would have given me some pleasure to tell him.

I said, "So basically you're the person who taught Wells all about time and radioactivity?"

"Well, I planted the seeds."

Then Elizabeth brought him and me back to the real question.

"Mr Hyatt. That is very interesting but how did you get here?"

He turned to her and said rather pompously, "You are very tenacious for a woman, Miss Bicester."

Oh dear. Time to hide under the table. I could tell by her expression that he was about to receive the full effect of her exposure to the twentieth century.

"Mr Hyatt. I should tell you I am Mrs Urquhart and a reminder to stick to the subject in question should not be interpreted as a weakness of my sex."

She then gave him a look which by his facial response indicated that in his youth a similar expression had possibly contributed to him hiding for the rest of his life in a boys only school.

___ ~ ___

E.

I must confess that the equality that James allows me, and that phrase says something of my upbringing, has given me a certain intolerance to references by men to the 'weaker sex'. However, since I have read the exploits of the suffragettes, I have felt a need to liberate men from their superiority when it is put on display. Though I should add, and I know this is not the case for all women, I am of the opinion that to supplant it with ours would significantly affect the pleasure of men's company.

Thankfully Mr Hyatt had recovered from my remark sufficiently to recount his story.

"I apologise, Mrs Urquhart. I had been headmaster at the grammar school at Midhurst since 1871. We had benefitted by the new Education Act to enlighten the poor. It was in 1880 I was first visited by Mr Wells, and this was the occasion when he showed me his books."

He paused for a moment as though he was trying to get something clear in his head then he continued, "There was also something else he showed me."

Again, a brief pause.

"Just as I thought he was about to leave he drew me to his carriage, opened the door and asked me to look inside. It was quite dark. At first, I thought it was just another passenger wrapped in a cloak or cover. As I stood there wondering to what purpose Mr Wells had brought me there the cloak seemed to fall away or dissolve to reveal the most wondrous creature. It was clad in a robe of saffron. At first, I thought it was a small man or boy but it had the face of what I can only describe as a rabbit! But that was of minor importance to what else I saw. It had wings, and the whole creature's skin, if that what is was, shone with an iridescent glow. Waves of colour, flushes of purple and crimson, golden green and intense blue seemed to cross its form. I was dumbstruck. It looked like an angel. I confess for a moment I thought my time had come. This feeling was reinforced when it turned to me and I felt myself falling into a strange sleep. However, instead of being transported to a place of God's choosing I found myself in a woodland clearing beside a stream. A strange glass object of pyramidal shape was before me and next to it stood Mr. Wells and the creature. This was beyond imagination. Then they beckoned me to enter. I could not resist despite all my mind wishing to leave! I passed through a translucent door and found myself in a small, metalled room in which I saw much machinery and two globes floating in the centre. As I looked at them in this dream like state, I thought one to be of the Earth and another, half its size, the colour of orange and blue.

The creature moved to the smaller one and indicated in my mind that that it was from whence it had come. Then Mr Wells operated some machinery and touched the larger globe. Suddenly, one wall dissolved to show the courtyard of an old house or Lodge. There I saw, what I now realise to be you and Mr Urquhart being met by an old man. Then the scene changed, and I was with Mr Urquhart and the person here who I now know was your father, Mr Bicester. They were both studying a strange sphere which I quickly realised was the same as the smaller orange globe in the pyramidal object. As I tried to understand what I saw the room dissolved and I was floating above the orange planet."

James interrupted, "Did you then have a vision of the destruction of the planet and how it turned orange, Mr Hyatt"

"Yes! Exactly. How did you know?"

"We've been to that planet and had the same visions."

"Good Lord! I do not know whether to be relieved or not. I have been questioning the state of my mind ever since and often thought it was a brain fever; that is until Mrs Urquhart's father arrived here."

I tried to reassure him a little and said, "I do understand it is difficult, Mr Hyatt. There have been many occasions that I have thought our adventures were just the dreams of a fevered mind. Our lives would have been much different - and quieter."

James retorted, "So we are both just apparitions of each other's deranged minds, Elizabeth?"

I let that thought go, "What happened after that?"

"I awoke to find myself back at the carriage of Mr Wells with his books. I was quite giddy at this point as you can imagine. He must have noticed for after enquiring after my heath asked me to recount what I had seen. I hesitated but after he asked whether I remember being in the strange object I told him quickly what I had seen.

"He was much relieved and then told me that I would be shortly in correspondence with his younger self and implored me once again to take him on and teach him all the sciences in the books he had given me. I was rather reticent as you can imagine. What wondrous child would this be?

"I asked why this was so important. He said it was to do with time itself. In order to bring a certain order to the world and save the two planets he had seen it was necessary for his younger self to have the advantage of an education of the future. It was especially important that I encourage the pupil to think about time and its fluidity. I must admit I was by now thoroughly confused and said I could not give a straight answer. He then became rather agitated and gripped my arm tightly and implored me to at least take the pupil on. He then produced a thick envelope and said it contained a thousand pounds which was mine if I took on this task. I promised I would take on this student though in my mind I had doubts that this child even existed."

"And did he?" said James.

"Yes, Mr Urquhart, he did! And he was a very keen scholar indeed."

"Did you tell him you had seen his future self?" I said.

"No. Mr Wells had stipulated that I should never recount what I had seen. However, I could plant in his mind the concept of the possible existence of angels from another world."

This story was incredible though seemed to dovetail into our own experiences. Yet there was a nagging uncertainty in my mind for I felt there were too many coincidences here. I tried to recall our journeys since we had decided to visit my home in the hope of making more sense of our situation. We had arrived at my house only to find we were back in 1873 but just after my father had left through the portal to look for us in the future. He had then found his way to Midhurst with the help of Jill where by chance met Mr Hyatt who was also out of his time and amazingly had been Mr Wells' tutor. Everything seemed very convenient. I decided to explore and turning to him said, "Although I am very pleased we have found you, Father, do you not think that you were incredibly lucky to find yourself here with another person of your time?"

He thought for a moment and replied, "I must admit, Lizzy, in hindsight some luck must have played its part and the fates were kind to us."

"I had not realised until now that you placed reliance on luck and the fates to guide you," goading him a little for he had always given me the impression of being a very practical man reliant on his own skills to make his way in the world.

He looked at me with that quizzical expression he used when he thought my interrogations of him were gaining advantage.

"I trust you are not implying that I have some complicity in this arrangement?"

I hesitated in answering his suggestion for I noticed he had said something which I had thought but not implied. But I kept that to myself and treading carefully so as not to arouse his suspicions of my purpose continued,

"I am just confused, Father, there just seemed to be too much luck involved."

But he had guessed my intention and deflected my remark easily, as only a father can do, back to me.

"So, Lizzy, too much luck, eh? But what of you and luck? Have you not had more than your fair share?"

I was taken aback. What did he mean? How much did he know about James and me and our adventures? A little flustered by his remark I blurted out, "What do you imply, Father?".

He saw my expression and relaxed with a smile back into his chair.

"Now let me see." He paused for a moment, a little too theatrically I thought, then looking me in the eyes said, "Ah yes. If I remember correctly I travelled to India expecting, you to be looking after the house. Instead, I find you have been gallivanting all over the place with this young man of questionable social standing and possibly both finding yourselves on occasion in intimate arrangements in the process which you may have found difficult to resist. Was it by luck or chance you found him or was it just fate? I do not wish to show disrespect to Mr Urquhart for I like him dearly and he is a good match for you, but he is not of the class you normally chase. Where did you really find him?"

I swear my cheeks turned redder than beetroot at that point not helped by the devilish smile my father put on when he noticed that he had successfully diverted me from my line of enquiry.

"Dear Lizzy, do not fret. When I've gone on, as they say, you may find some diaries of my own in the Lodge from my youth where you might be surprised to learn I did not spend the entire time in a monastic existence."

Although I was gratified to hear his reply, I did not feel much change in the colour of my face. For, I must say it is difficult for a single lady in the company of men to have her moral predicament discussed so plainly, nor to contemplate her father being so fully cognisant because he has participated in similar activity - and kept a record which he was inviting me to read after his death!

Thankfully James, who was looking a little embarrassed as well, came to the rescue by changing the subject or more importantly not.

"Ok. I've got that," he said, "but I think Elizabeth asked how did you get here in this time?"

--- ~ ---

J.

I could see that Elizabeth's father in future was going to get some humorous mileage out of our relationship at our expense now he knew what we'd been up to. However, I made a mental note to absorb it without too much comment whenever the subject came our way.

Hyatt had still not told us how he got here. It seems when people get to a certain age, in telling a story they have difficulty getting to the end of it and are easily distracted from its path by the simplest interruption. Oh dear. I'm doing the same here. To the point, Urquhart!

So to summarise: Hyatt arrived here in Midhurst five days ago, not weeks, brought in a time machine provided by Wells. Why? To meet Elizabeth's father. Why? Because Elizabeth's father is going to meet me in 1873 and show me the Martian canals and tell me about the little folk who live on Harrow Hill. Simple really. It's so much easier to understand when one is brief. Isn't it? No.

There was one point missing, "What year was it when Wells brought you here? If you understand what I mean."

"1895."

Of course. The year Wells published 'The Time Machine'. Then I remembered Mr Hyatt's reference to the creature in the carriage in 1880 and his likening it to an angel. This had some familiarity. I looked it up on my phone which recently I had increasing difficulty keeping out of Elizabeth hands (must buy her one) and eventually found that Wells had produced a book called "The Wonderful Visit" in which he describes such a creature! It seems some welsh vicar, not understanding what it was, had shot and wounded it. Welcome to Earth. Then I remembered that in another time line, 'The War of the Worlds' had been started by just such a thing.

"So now you've met Mr Bicester," I said, "What are you supposed to do now?"

"Why, I must go back and drop off him off, so to speak, at his home just before you arrive to meet him for the first time."

"And pray tell me, how?" said Elizabeth.

"Why, in Mr Wells' Time Machine."

Elizabeth and I nearly fell off our chairs.

"What? Are you saying there is a time machine around here?"

"Of course," he said, "How else could I get back to my own time?" He gave a look indicating that he was stating the obvious.

When I had recovered, I said, "Ok, where is it?"

"It is on the old castle field. Do you wish to see it?"

--- ~ ---

Chapter Four

E,

The four of us walked down the road to the castle hill. Two people in modern dress, one wearing James' suite and another in an 1880's frock coat. We tried not to notice whether we were being noticed but I had the distinct impression that everyone we met on Church Road did notice. This feeling was not helped by one of us in a modern short dress being the subject of some comment about her attire by her father.

"Do you not feel a little too exposed, Lizzy?"

I was wearing a blouse and a skirt which came just below the knee. I had done up the top buttons of my blouse in deference to my father. James and his sister had often ribbed me about the length of my dress but having been brought up where even the sight of an ankle or calf was to invite a certain type of notice I had resisted their banter. This was despite James trying to persuade me that I had the best legs in Sussex and should show them off whenever possible. How fashions change.

Nevertheless I tried to reassure my father by replying, "I can only say that in this modern world my choice of clothing is often likened to a schoolteacher or vicar's daughter by our friends."

"Be that as it may Lizzy. I'm not convinced the Reverend Newcomb at Finworth would approve of his daughter so dressed. Mind you he does keep her on a very tight rein and always buttoned up."

I decided not to mention that the Reverend 's daughter, Jane, far from being 'buttoned up' was often found 'unbuttoned' if I might be so bold, on Friday evenings at a certain Mrs Faversham's home in Midhurst. We had attended one of these soirees and afterwards and in fact for some days after, James commented that he was surprised on the variety of stockings ladies wore in my time. Despite his generous offers to pay a return visit at his expense I resisted as I thought too much exposure to such hosiery would affect his health. His suggestion that perhaps I might jealously think he would run off with one of those strumpets was denied emphatically.

However, luckily for my modesty, for much of the promenade to the castle James distracted us by trying to understand the implications of what we were going to do.

--- ~ ---

J.

I was still having some difficulty trying to get my head around the time loop that Wells had put Elizabeth's father in. The first time I met him was in 1873 in the courtyard of Hamgreen when he said he had just come back from India after being delayed about two weeks in the Mediterranean. The second time was today, but today Hyatt is going to take him back to Hamgreen. I asked where and more importantly to 'when' he was taking him. Elizabeth's father answered instead.

"We have decided for continuity and to minimise disturbance that I am taken back to the time I was about to go to India."

"But surely you would meet yourself?"

"I thought that to," interrupted Hyatt, "but Mr Wells said that it was impossible because, if I repeat the words correctly, a person cannot occupy the same time state. I'm not sure what that means."

I said, "Perhaps it means that if you go back or forward in time then you take over yourself at that point."

Elizabeth said, "So you are suggesting that if I went back to say 1870 to where I was living, I would become the person who occupies myself at that time. But surely people would notice because I would appear about three years older. That does not seem logical."

"I know but Wells went back to see Mr Hyatt at the time when Wells was only a pupil and Wells was much older."

"So, if my father returns to 1873 to go to India, what happens to my father who is already there? Does he just disappear?"

This just didn't make sense then I remembered the time slips and the different world's we'd been in.

"OK, how about this." I said, "We have parallel world's or timelines. Each time we travel back or forward in time there is a slight aberration and for the most part we end in a parallel world which is so similar that we do not notice the change."

"Yes, I remember," said Elizabeth, "We has long discussions with Jill on the matter for on certain occasions we ended up on a parallel world which was some distance from ours. This one for instance James which is in many ways different from the world's we left when we first met."

"Yes, I think that is the clue."

"So you are saying that when my father goes back in time to Hamgreen he will, oh how should I put it, oh yes, he slots into a slightly different time line where the person who is him ceases to exist at the point of his materialisation."

"Well put." I said. "Though I'm not quite sure what makes the other self-dematerialise as you put it but I like the theory.

However, it looks like we are going to find out shortly. Here's the church lane to the castle"

--- ~ ---

E.

As we passed the nave and walked into the overgrown field where the remains of the castle lay I wondered whether the souterrain and the cavern still existed beneath us and what was now in it.   But my thoughts were quickly interrupted for there, slightly hidden in the shrubbery, before us was the device. It was strangest thing I had ever seen.

It had the shape of a pyramidal bell as described by Mr Hyatt and laying at an angle on its side. The surface seemed to be made of plates of a glasslike substance held by a frame in much the same way as the stained glass in a church is held in place. Mr Hyatt walked over to it and touched the surface which caused one of the plates to open revealing a dark entrance.

"Well here we are Mr Bicester. Are you ready to go back home?"

My father said, " I'm afraid I do not have many options to the contrary. What little of this world I have seen although fascinating is too out of place for me."

I felt something was wrong. It was too simple. I tried to understand what would happen. Then it came to me. I said, "Just a minute Mr Hyatt. We came here to take my father back to his home. Now you are taking him back. If we go home to Hamgreen without him what will become of him?"

My father came up to me and holding my hand said, "Don't worry Lizzy. You will see me soon."

41

"How?" I said with not a little worry.

"We will meet at the Lodge at another time."

And before I could express my concern he turned and accompanied Mr Hyatt into the machine.

I looked at James. He also had a very worried expression upon his face. He saw the concern in my face and said, "I don't understand either. What does he mean, another time?"

"I am at a loss also." I said. "But I believe what he says. Though I must admit my belief is more in hope than conviction."

Suddenly the time machine seemed to shiver. Then it vanished.

I turned to James who was still looking at the now empty patch in the shrubbery. "Do you think father will be alright?"

"I wish I could reassure you but all I can think of doing is going back to your home and see if he turns up there. Shall we go?"

I could not think of a better plan, so I agreed but I was reluctant to leave. But as we turned and walked away I heard a faint sound behind us. I looked back.

"James!" I cried, "The machine has reappeared!"

As we watched it materialise the door started to open and out of the hatch stepped Mr Batalia!

"Quick! Hide!" Shouted James and pulled me quite roughly into the bushes.

Unfortunately, at the same moment James phone sounded a bell followed by a number of words by James which would not normally be said in the presence of a lady.

But before I could say anything he answered it. It was Jill.

"Where are you, Jim? I thought you'd be here."

"I'm in Midhurst," he whispered forcefully.

"Why are you whispering Jim?"

"It's all gone to Hell! Elizabeth's father has been whisked off in a time machine to God knows where and it's just come back with Marco minus Elizabeth's father."

"You mean Marco 's turned up again? Tell Elizabeth to stab him with that hat pin of hers for me."

I would have gladly carried out her wishes if I had one. But I noticed Mr Batalia was now coming towards us. I nudged James to warn him.

"I've got to go Jill." he said, "Jill, do me a favour. Drive up to Hamgreen and tell Flory what's happened."

"Flory is here?"

"No! She's still back in the 1870's"

"What? You want me to travel back in time. How? Don't tell me it involves sitting in a submerged black box with a bucket for a friend again."

I could see that this conversation between siblings was going nowhere. I grabbed the phone off James, rather rudely I confess but needs must, and spoke to Jill.

When I had finished there was a moment of silence on the phone. Then Jill said, "OK Elizabeth. I think I've got it. I take some of your Victorian clothes and hiking gear from Chichester, go to Hamgreen, jump through a time portal and meet Flory in the nineteenth century and tell her what's happened. Can't see a problem. Just a normal day. Did Jim get you into this or have you been taking his pills?"

"No Jill. I am afraid it was all the fault of my curiosity."

Before I could continue, James grabbed the phone back and said, "Good luck Sis," and closed the phone.

Mr Batalia was now no more than thirty yards from us. James said, "I don't think he's spotted us yet. Let's work our way around this undergrowth and see if we can get to that machine."

Before I could answer James was off into the undergrowth and I found myself crawling on all fours through shrubbery which seemed to contain more than its fair share of brambles and nettles and reminded me very much of our exploits at Newgrange, except at that place I was blessed with a full covering of Victorian clothing. Here I had nothing but a light blouse and a short cotton skirt. Luckily, I was not wearing stocking otherwise I would have emerged with the appearance of a trollop after a 'successful' evening in North Park. Not, I should add for anyone who may read this, have I been to North Park of an evening and seen one.

We emerged from the bushes still on all fours by the machine. I could see Mr Batalia by an old oak towards the church but unfortunately, he had also spotted our position as well and by the way he ran towards us I could see he had guessed our intent.

"Now," said James, "Run!"

I needed no encouragement despite the pain of the stinging nettles on my arms and legs. We clambered through the hatch of the machine and fell to the floor. James immediately grabbed the door and pulled it closed. There were two bolts which he quickly drew across the door to seal it. It was not a moment too soon for as he slid across the last bolt I heard Mr Batalia 's efforts to open the door.

--- ∼ ---

J.

After about five minutes the banging on the door stopped and there was no further sound.

I said, "I hope he's gone away and not still trying to access or disable this machine."

However, Elizabeth was more concerned about drawing my attention to herself. I made the mistake of asking if she was alright.

"James, I am cut and stung to blazes and my blouse and skirt which I only bought on Saturday at some expense are now shredded. I have the appearance of a person who has had an altercation with a large cat and has come off worse."

"Well, I'm in not much better state myself."

For some reason this attention to myself did not provoke the concern I was expecting. Luckily, I have learnt with the fairer sex that the response I received was a clear signal to take a different tact quickly and dose it with liberal quantities of sympathy and humility. After adopting such a path for about five minutes my nearest and dearest eventually agreed that perhaps our actions were the best in the circumstances.

" So what do we do now?" She said, still trying to rearrange her clothes into some semblance of Victorian modesty and accidently revealing a rather nice pair of thighs in the process which I thought it best not to compliment her on them at that moment.

"I think we'll see if we can get this machine working then go back to meet Jill and Flory."

"And what of my father? You do remember the whole purpose of this adventure was to find him?"

Her tone indicated a little more mollification was still required.

"I DO remember Elizabeth." I said, "I can only suggest that as Hyatt said he was taking your father back to your home in 1873 he might be there."

She thought for a minute then said, "I have to agree. For

I can't think of anything else that might meet with success. And if we are wrong we might be able to use this machine to try some time else."

"There's one problem though. If we go back to the time when we last met Flory, will the time portal still be there in the doorway?"

"If it is we must deal with it. We will only find out by going there."

"OK. Let's try it." Then I said with a smile, "There's a small bonus though. We've now managed to steal two-time machines from Marco and left him stranded in time twice. Not bad eh for a couple who haven't a clue what they're doing."

--- ~ ---

Chapter Five

E.

The controls in the time machine were similar to the ones we had seen in the cavern, when dealing with the Martians. As before, there were two globes. James carefully and slowly moved the pointer on the globe that depicted the Earth and I watched the scene on the wall as we floated down the roads to Hamgreen and then into the drive.

James said, " Right. I've got the machine into the courtyard but I think we are still in 2016. We now have to decide whether we get out now and go through the time portal in the door of the lodge or we somehow take this machine back to 1873."

I said, "I suppose much will depend on what point in time we wish to arrive. Do we go back to just before my father left the house and stop him?"

"I like the idea. If we stop him, he can't meet Hyatt and he doesn't get into the machine."

"But does that mean he doesn't show you the map of Mars?"

"I don't know, Elizabeth."

This did seem a quandary, then something quite worrying occurred to me which helped me make up my mind.

I said, "I have just thought. We are in 2016 still. We have not travelled in time. Mr Batalia may have concluded we are here and is on his way to find us!"

"Damn! You're right. If I was him stuck without a time machine, I think I'd try this place first. He could be here in minutes! Let's get back to 1873 when we left Flory."

This conclusion made sense, if sense was allowed in this

argument, and I agreed. James adjusted the chronometers to that time. As he did so the scene on the wall became a flickering blur. Trees and shrubs changed shape or disappeared. We slowed suddenly into an autumn scene. The leaves had turned and many had fallen leaving a thick yellow and orange carpet on the ground.

James shut down the machine and the vision vanished from the wall, "Well, we've got rid of Marco. Let's go and see who's at the door."

I was not looking forward to this, not least because of my appearance. I hoped whoever came to the door recognised us and didn't see us off as a pair of ragamuffins.

I pulled the bell and after what seemed a long wait the door opened. There was no blank wall, just Flory.

"Oh, Elizabeth, you are back again!"

The way she spoke indicated that we had been here recently. James said, "Sorry, we keep on getting stuck in and out of time. When we were last here? I mean exactly, do you know the date when my sister Jill arrived?"

This was rather devious of James, but I knew what he was doing.

"Why, it is not a week since," said Flory, "Last Saturday, you remember, don't you?"

I realised we must be a week ahead of our last visit and said, "Oh yes, of course. Please excuse us, we have to go!"

"Where are you going?" She said, looking rather frightened, "Did you find Father?"

"No. I'm sorry but that is why we have to go now." I said rather sorrowfully for I could see she was in some distress.

We quickly said goodbye to my now rather confused sister and re-entered the machine.

"I hope you didn't mind my rudeness, Elizabeth?" said

James.

"No. I understand. Shall we go back to last Saturday and start again?"

Once again James adjusted the controls to the previous week. The scene on the wall looked virtually the same. When the date arrived on the counting device we disembarked and went across the courtyard to the door again. I could feel the cold autumn air on my skin.

Flory answered the door. There was still no portal. Or so we thought.

"Oh, you are back quickly. Did you find Father?"

I replied, "We did but we lost him. Can we come in, it is rather cold here?"

Flory looked at me and then my clothes. "I'm not surprised. What happened to you? And why are you just in those ragged undergarments, Elizabeth?"

Before I could answer, she said, "Wait there a minute I will be back shortly," and vanished into the house while we stood in the cold.

She returned, just before we were about to give up, with one of my red afternoon dresses. "Put this on quick. Otherwise, Henry will have a fit."

While I struggled to put on the dress over my skirt and blouse she turned to James and surveyed his apparel. "I cannot do anything for you, James. You will have to do the best you can as you are."

--- ~ ---

J.

We entered the hall. I was conscious, after looking at my clothes that compared to the girls I now looked like some

49

farm labourer in one of Thomas Hardy's books. Elizabeth reinforced this impression by carefully removing some vegetation from my hair and jacket and saying,

"There, James. You are much improved and almost as good as when you first met me at that cricket match."

Flory looked at me and then Elizabeth and with a giggle said, "Yes, it is a mystery why you did not fall head over heels in love with him immediately on that occasion."

"Are you suggesting that my attire on that fateful day was not sufficient to bowl a maiden over at first look?" I said pretending to be offended and at the same time, congratulating myself in getting a cricket term in.

"I'm sure a maiden would have been," whispered Flory to Elizabeth. They looked at each other in mock horror before breaking into a fit of the giggles. Do these women have no shame? I looked at the ceiling and whistled under my breath, until they had regained control of themselves.

Flory finally gasped out. "Cheer up, James. Henry will understand that you have been in yet another escapade which accounts for your appearance."

We went into the study where Henry was standing by the fireplace. He looked at me with surprise then recovered.

"It is gratifying to see you both, but I notice you are without my uncle."

We told them the whole story including our escape from Marco.

"It is a pity you couldn't persuade him to come with you."

I was about to protest but he stopped me with a sympathetic response. "But then often in hindsight, Mr Urquhart, the right decisions appear much easier."

"Thanks, Henry," I said, "but this might sound a bit strange but can you tell us what's today's date is?"

"It is the 14th of October."

"And the year?"

"Why, it is 1873!" he replied, giving a puzzled glance to Flory.

A bell rang in the hall. Flory and Henry looked at each other again. Flory said, "There is someone at the front door."

She was hesitant. No one moved so I volunteered to go with her. I hoped it wasn't Marco. I pulled back the bolts and Flory unlocked the door. I opened it slowly. Nothing! I was confronted with the blank portal time-wall again. Summoning a bit more nerve than I really had in front of Flory I then peered through it. The scream was quite piercing.

"Bloody Hell, Jim!" said Jill, "What are you trying to do to me? And why are you floating there like a ghost without a body?"

My brain was on overdrive. When we went back last time we had lost a week so she should not have arrived here for another seven days.

"What are you doing here?"

"You told me to come - remember?"

"But that was in a week's time!"

"What are you talking about? It was this afternoon."

This was beyond me. I said, "Get your stuff from the car Jill and get in here as quick as you can."

She gave me a questioning look that I'm sure she usually reserved for the criminally insane then ran to the car and retrieved a large bag from the boot. When she returned, she said. "OK, Jim, how do I get in? All I can see is a blank wall with your decapitated creepy head sticking out of it."

"Just walk through as though it isn't there."

"What? Why? What's on the other side?"

"Just do it!"

She closed her eyes and made a lunge for the door. Unfortunately, because the portal did not have any physical resistance she crashed through at some speed and bowled us over like nine pins. When we all got back on our feet Jill said, "Where am I? It's blooming freezing...Oh hello Flory what are you doing here... My God! I really am in the nineteenth century, aren't I?"

Flory's shocked face made Jill look down at her own clothing. She tugged uselessly at the hem of her tight, sleeveless, and very short dress. What really concerned me though was when I had looked out into the court yard the time machine was not there. But then I realised of course out there was 2016.

$$--- \sim ---$$

E.

I went to the hall to see what was causing the commotion followed closely by Henry who had grabbed a large poker from the fireplace.

I took one look at Jill's attire but before I could say anything, behind me I heard Henry exclaim, "Good God, woman! Go upstairs and dress yourself immediately," and he retired back into the study.

James just managed to get his hand across Jill's mouth in time before she replied and then tried to convince her, without much success, that no further sensible conversation was going to happen until she was dressed in a more modest style.

A little heated discussion concerning men, their double

standards and ladies' fashions followed which I could see James thought it wise not to participate in.

Eventually Jill said resignedly, "OK. I'll do it but I'm NOT going to force myself into one of those bloomin' corsets again just to turn on your cousin?"

As I had 'given up' the dreadful things some time ago she had my sympathy. As to 'turning on' Henry, if I understood it to mean what I thought it meant, it was best left alone and I said,

"No, Jill. Just a bit of modesty is required. You can keep your clothes on underneath."

I still remember James showing me pictures of the compressed torsos of ladies who had been subjected to a lifetime of corsets purely to follow fashion. Not to mention the constrictions to the lungs which must have contributed greatly to the ease with which women fainted, and no doubt reinforced the idea that we were the weaker sex.

Eventually Jill agreed and Flory took her upstairs while James and I returned to the study where Henry was standing facing the fire. When he heard us he turned and said, "I make no apology for my exclamation though perhaps I could have said it with less haste. But here in this world there are certain conventions to which I insist you adhere; not least to protect the servants and Flory."

___ ~ ___

J.

I was about to challenge him on his remark but he stopped me in my tracks.

"Mr Urquhart, I know you have been with my cousin for some time and I believe you are an honest man but I hear you have been living, how should I say, in close proximity. Do you not think you could make an honest woman of her?"

"But Henry, we are married!" Elizabeth said.

He looked at us rather incredulously then said, "Yes. But that is in the future. Here you are in a time before your marriage and I suggest that if you are residing here overnight then, for the sake of the servants, I would prefer if you slept in separate bedrooms."

I decided not to protest though Elizabeth gave me a look indicating I was not sufficiently defending her honour. Instead I replied,

"Look, our priority is to find Elizabeth's father. And I'm afraid to say we also have to find Marco because he came out of the machine Elizabeth's father entered. There is a problem though."

"What do you mean?" said Henry and Elizabeth almost in unison.

"We have lost the time machine."

Henry gave me a look I'm sure he reserved only for a servant who had provided him with the wrong club on the golf course and said, "Do you mean to tell me that you have not only lost my cousin's father but also the means of finding him?"

Before I could answer he turned despairingly to Elizabeth and said, "I thought this was a man in which you placed great trust, Elizabeth?"

"I do trust him, Henry. But I think this adventure would be exceedingly trying even for you!" She stormed out of the room leaving me alone with her cousin.

There's nothing like a bit of stress to get people arguing about the wrong things. I motioned Henry to sit down and preferably as far away from the blunt instruments in the fire place as possible then tried to explain to him that we had come from the year 2016 to 1873 via the machine. But now if we tried to leave, the time portal meant the world outside the front door leads to the future again.

Eventually I got him to understand what we were up against and he admitted that used as he was to looking after the Bicester estates and two precocious female cousins, he now could see our situation would test even his limits.

--- ~ ---

E.

On leaving Henry I went upstairs to join Flory and Jill where I have to say the discussion on corsets, men and morals continued for a little while. Then just as we were complimenting ourselves on how sensible women were, Flory said, "Jill, what do you mean by turning Henry on?"

I had previously suspected that Henry and Flory were very close but thought nothing of it, until now.

Jill said in her usual and normally endearing fashion, "I presume the sight of a woman underdressed in front a Victorian man is going to get him rather aroused."

Flory with her cheeks now blushing a little replied a little tartly, "I can assure you Henry is not that kind of man and would certainly not be distracted by such an apparition."

Jill looked at me, and seeing my expression indicated I had reached the same conclusion as she had, she quickly changed the subject and said, "Sorry, Flory. Please forgive my language. I'm still recovering from being transported here and seeing Jim's face poking through that door."

Then the thought of James' head floating in the air caused

us all to laugh and thankfully brought us back together again. Dear James, he does bring brightness to my life in so many ways. However, I will watch Henry and Flory with renewed interest in future.

Once we were satisfied that Jill was "respectable" we returned to the menfolk who seemed now the best of friends and were busy scribbling on a tablecloth. When they saw us they ignored the work we had done on Jill and instead drew our attention immediately to the cloth which had a rough drawing of the plan of the lodge with arrows going in all directions.

They were discussing whether we should stay in this time without the machine or return to the future without it.

It seemed an impasse. How were we going to find Father? While looking at their drawing I remembered that when Henry and Flory had left the Lodge by the rear entrance they remained in their world. This gave a possible solution, and I said, "I have an idea. If you will all follow me?"

They all looked at me and no doubt concluding that I had a touch of the vapours due to a too tight a corset decided to humour me and followed me through the kitchens and out into the garden.

--- ~ ---

J.

I had never been in a real Victorian garden before. I had some idea from the paintings of Monet and Leighton but to see a real one was a dream. It was full of autumn flowers. Masses of marigolds, daisies and chrysanthemums spread over the box hedge and wild roses clambered up the trellises and disappeared into the tightly clipped yew hedge.

This was still a time when nature was in equal competition with man and the flora displayed was determined by nature and not the local garden centre. I asked Elizabeth, as I followed her down the green path, if we ever get back to a normal world together whether she thought a year of hard work by me might turn our home and small patch into an enchantment like this?

She turned to me and holding my hand said, "James, you are my enchantment. But if you wish we will make a garden together where you can enchant me forever."

That was a bit too much even by my romantic standards and she noticed a tear fall from my eye.

"James! Are you crying? You fool." And she kissed me.

I had to sit down for a moment. A cricket buzzed near me in the grass and landed on my hand and a late butterfly rose from the last flower on a buddleia and passed over my head. If there was a fairy land it was here. I thought back to that fateful day with my friends rambling in the Sussex countryside when I was distracted by that butterfly in the woods and found myself in her world at Hamgreen. Did that butterfly know what it was doing and drew me to her?

For some reason an image of a small, winged Martian came into my head. But before I could pursue that thought we had left the garden and turned around the side of the Lodge.

And there in the courtyard was the time machine. Why didn't I think of that?

I said to Elizabeth, "Of course! It's only if you go through the portal that time changes."

She then said with a twinkle in her eye, "I would wager that if we had gone out through the front door to 2016 and then went around the back of the house it would still be the same time."

I don't know why she goes out with me. It was so obvious.

"Well, "I replied, swallowing my pride, "there is only one way to find out."

So we encouraged everyone to join us and we all went around the back of the house again, re-entered the kitchen and exited out of the front door into 2016.

Then we returned to the back again. By now Flory, Henry and Jill were beginning to think we had lost our marbles and all hope of finding a certain father would have to be abandoned. However, when we entered the kitchen this time, much respect for the intrepid adventurers was restored. For luckily we were confronted with a kitchen of the future with all the electric gadgets of its time. We were so pleased with our deductions that when we entered the study and Henry and Flory started exclaiming about the television and the hi-fi equipment we did not at first notice Marco sitting in the armchair by the window.

--- ~ ---

Chapter Six

E.

The shock of seeing Mr Batalia was almost matched by the shock of Henry grabbing him by his collar and lifting him out of his seat and shouting into his face in a most threatening manner.

"What are you doing here? I thought I left you up at Midhurst! Are you after my cousin again?"

Mr Batalia was surprisingly quite unfazed by this outburst though I noticed he was regarding James and me quite closely. He said very calmly, "And I may ask what are you all doing here?"

"It is YOU who is an intruder in my house!" I shouted rather louder than I expected.

"I think you'll find that you're the intruders because it's my house. I'm renting it from one of your sister's grandchildren."

We were all dumbfounded. Not least Flory who had collapsed in a half faint into Henry's arms. How did our house end up in the hands of Mr Batalia?

No one spoke. Seeing that his comment had had the intended effect on us he continued. "I've come to take you two to your father. He's with Wells and his old tutor Hyatt."

Eventually James broke the silence, "And what does Wells want to do with him, Marco? That's if what you're saying is true - which I very much doubt."

"Wells needs Mrs Urquhart's father to show you the canals of Mars."

This was indeed what Mr Hyatt had said but before I could speak James asked my question in his own way.

"Yes, I've got that, Marco, but what's it got to do with you? And also how did you get into their time machine? Because last time we saw you we left you in 2015 at Newgrange."

This was a conundrum. We had heard nothing concerning him after that until his sudden appearance from the time machine at Midhurst. Until then I had presumed he had either entered the burial chamber at Newgrange or the observatory hidden in the bushes and was lost in some other time line or on Mars.

Mr Batlaia replied rather hotly to James' enquiry. "Yes, you did leave me at Newgrange. Didn't even offer me a lift."

"Don't give me that!" retorted James, "You had already disappeared. Where did you go?" said James.

"Why, I returned to the cavern at Midhurst."

"So how did you find Wells' time machine?" said James getting angrier than was good for him.

"I didn't find it - I made it for him."

This pushed us back on the defensive. "What? How?" I heard myself say, trying to comprehend him.

"From the machine you left me. of course. Remember you sent me off to 2016 and shut down the power supplies."

"Yes," said James trying to control his emotions. "So you should be trapped in 2016 but obviously you found a way out"

"Obviously. You see, you left me an intact time machine. All I needed was a new power source. So when I got back to the cavern I went through the portal to the derelict Martian fleet and removed one of their power sources. A fusion reactor can be quite small if you can find the right material to generate and contain an appropriately strong magnetic field. Oh yes, and if it occupies a five dimensional space."

I looked at James for assistance for this was beyond my knowledge. His eyes were screwed tightly, deep in thought. I gently nudged him.

He saw my expression and after a moment said, "So Marco, are you saying that a small fusion power source can be made if you spread its power density out along a fourth dimension like time for instance?"

"Right in one. You were always quite clever, Urquhart, for just a science teacher. Weren't you?"

I held James' arm tightly.

Mr Batalia finding that his remark had fallen on barren ground continued, "Its power density cannot be contained in just normal three-dimensional space but if you can spread a little bit into the past and future you can dilute it so that in any point in three-dimensional space it can be easily contained."

"And you need to be able to see in five dimensions in order to see the fourth, like the Martians," replied James.

"Precisely."

Once again James had been able to make a deduction and reduce its components to a simplicity which allowed me to comprehend it. However, these facts although important did not answer why Mr Batalia was involved with Mr Wells and my father.

"Mr Batalia, why are you here and where is my father?"

"I told you he is with Wells in 1895 and safe. I am really here because at the cavern I found there is an end to time."

--- ~ ---

J.

Marco 's last statement had us all stunned.

Eventually I said, "How do you know?"

"I discovered it at the cavern while looking at the sky screens. Have you looked at the stars recently?"

He could see we didn't understand what he was getting at.

Henry, having laid Flory on a chaise longue, took his comment seriously and went to the window. It was now after sunset. He said, "I see stars, Mr Batalia. What of it?"

"Yes, but it is what you can't see is the problem."

"And what can't I see? The sky is clear."

"OK. Let me explain for it's very obvious. When you look out the window at the sky at night as I'm sure you often do, you are looking at the past."

A glimmer of where this was leading entered my head but I let him continue.

"The nearest star is about four light years away so when we look at it we are seeing what it was four years ago."

Henry interjected. "This light year? I have heard it used by my uncle. Is it not the distance light can travel in a year?"

"Yes. You are well informed. Now the galaxies beyond the Milky Way such as Andromeda are millions of light years away."

"That is fantasy! And what is this Milky Way or galaxies to use your Greek? The universe of which I have read is believed to be only a few thousands of these light years across."

"I'm afraid not, Henry," I said, "Our galaxy in which we live is just one of millions of galaxies which occupy the Universe."

"Poppycock! Why would God make it so large?"

It was a good point.

I said, "No one really knows, Henry. But scientists say," divorcing myself from my own profession in the hope of giving him a better understanding, "that they can see objects whose light left them over ten thousand million years ago. It is really, really big."

I could see Henry was struggling with this. I hoped he didn't believe in Bishop Usher's age of the world as four and half thousand years.

I turned back to Marco, "So what makes you think that time has an end?"

He looked at me with an almost sardonic grin and said, "Let's try a little experiment. I happen to have your wife's father's telescope in the conservatory."

We followed him through the hall and gathered together in the room where Elizabeth's father had originally kept his telescope, and we had looked together at Mars.

"Now, Urquhart, I'm sure you know where the Andromeda galaxy is. Perhaps you can show it to us through the telescope."

I opened a window and quickly found the great square of Pegasus above the horizon. I turned the telescope towards it, then a little left searching for the faint glow of the galaxy. The sky was clear, yet I couldn't see it. I checked the lens cap wasn't on as I had happened on one or two occasions to the delight of my students at college and the embarrassment to myself.

I tried again. Points of starlight drifted across my view, but I still could not find Andromeda.

I looked at the sky again with my own eyes just to confirm there were no clouds. The sky was crystal clear and black. There was no galaxy. This was worrying. I could usually see it as a faint smudge even with the naked eye.

"Where's it gone?" I said to no one in particular which was rather a stupid question.

"Oh, I'm sure it still there, Urquhart," said Marco, "But as you know the light from Andromeda takes a two and a half million years to get here."

I thought I began to see what he was driving at.

"You mean the light from it is no longer reaching us? Has it exploded? I would have thought a galaxy that close going nova would light up the sky. Or has it somehow just imploded into itself and vanished?"

"You're on the wrong track. Keep thinking, Urquhart."

As I tried to think whilst ignoring the urge to punch his goading face, Elizabeth said, "Are you saying, Mr Batalia, that the past now only stretches back to a certain time?"

"Well done, Mrs Urquhart. You have it."

I knew I shouldn't have taught her all that stuff on Relativity. I whispered into her ear. "You know my next wife is going to be kept in the kitchen making cakes and having babies."

To which she whispered back, "You only have to ask your present wife, and you may find she could become quite competent in those skills as well."

I filed away that offer away very carefully for future use.

Elizabeth had got to the nub of it. I now realised what he meant by the end of time.

The real question now was, how far in the past could we now see? I looked out the window and my fears were confirmed. Even the Milky Way had vanished!

"Yes, Urquhart. The fourth dimension seems to have become finite!"

I asked the only question, "Do you think it's getting shorter?"

"I don't know. I phoned Jodrell Bank but got no answer. And before you look, there's nothing on the Internet about it."

"Which means everyone in authority knows."

"Or no one knows they exist."

Elizabeth said, "Yes, I see what you mean. Perhaps in this timeline we are in the Milky Way has never existed or the light from it has not, or cannot, reach us."

"Quite possible. Either way it means we're on our own."

"What do you mean 'we', Marco?" I said.

Before he could reply, Jill said, "I'm lost here. What's the milky way? Sounds more like an industrial dairy farm to me than a group of stars."

"You know," said Marco, "The band of stars which makes up our galaxy."

"What are you talking about? Show me," said Jill, looking distinctly un-nerved.

"I can't. It's not there."

"So you're telling me," she said with some annoyance in her voice, "there's a thing out there called the Milky Way in the sky which you can't see. What are you playing at, Marco?"

Then getting no reply she turned to the rest of us. "Does anybody know what he's talking about?"

___~___

E.

A cold clammy streak ran down my back. I realised that the world in which we now were since emerging from the white cliffs was more different to our previous world than I had thought. In this Jill's world the Universe was a smaller place. I had to protect my friend.

"Jill, you should know Mr Batalia is always playing with us. You should not take him too seriously."

"What are you talking about, Miss Bicester?" said Mr Batalia in his usual brusque manner.

"It is Mrs Urquhart." I reminded him.

"Yea. Whatever," he replied rather rudely then turning to Jill said, "Basically, Miss Urquhart, you're in a timeline where most of your universe is missing. But I expect you don't know that."

I was about to come to Jill's defence when I was pleased to see she could manage on her own.

She said, "Yes, I do, Marco. I know I exist in many timelines, as do we all. For example, in one line Elizabeth is pregnant. In another I've never seen a computer. In this world I've never seen this Milky Way, whatever it is. The thing is, Marco, how many Marcos do you think you are?"

Mr Batalia looked quite shocked.

"There's only one of me!"

"You wish. I bet there's hundreds of Marcos running around and trying to change time to their advantage. But as far as I can tell they all keep failing."

I loved the way Jill is able to cut to the quick with such ease. Sometimes I have wished I could abandon the baggage of my society to allow me to speak more plainly when required but apparently James assures me I can manage it quite successfully when the need arises.

Having silenced Mr Batalia, Jill continued. "But enough of you. This all looks too serious. I need to get Sean and tell him what's going on."

I said, "Are you sure that's a good idea? It's a lot to take in."

"He's from Kerry, remember. He thinks he's been surrounded by the fairy folk all his life."

I couldn't fault what she said. When you are with Jill's husband, Sean, strange things happen. The west coast of Ireland where he is from is a magical place. I remember James and I had been looking for a time portal at Dunbeg Fort near Dingle. We had become lost and called on a cottage for guidance. When we asked the occupant if she knew its location she crossed herself and said she knew the place, but we should be careful as it was occupied by the Sidhe. But that is another story. I did not want Jill going off on her own and suggested, "I would rather you stayed here than go out there on your own. Tell him you are at Hamgreen without transport and need assistance. But don't mention what we found until he gets here. I am sure on hearing your predicament that he will be here in a thrice."

"No, Elizabeth. If he comes here and sees a severed head poking out that door, with his Irish background he's going to think Cuchulainn and his horde are inside and he won't stop running till he gets to Dingle. And besides," she said, looking at James, "I don't want to find myself stuck in another time tub."

I could see that the event at Loch Ness with James was never going to go away no matter what time line we were in. However, I was still trying to understand how the past was vanishing. Was it just a dimension or did it include what we remembered? I asked everyone if they would indulge me in a little test.

They nodded.

I said, "How far back can you remember in history? Can anyone remember when the Romans left Britain?"

"Who are the Romans?" James said.

They all looked at him in disbelief.

"No, I'm only kidding. Around 400 AD I think."

"That is not funny, James. Now be serious. What about dinosaurs? They were millions of years ago."

James said, "Yep. Remember them. So if I get your drift it looks like our brains are not affected."

"So," I said rather cautiously for my grasp of this subject was very tenuous, "What's the effect of this edge of time?"

Marco said, "For some reason it has become finite in length. It is acting like a spatial dimension. For all I know it's getting shorter. There was a time when we could see the Milky Way. Now it's gone."

"But was that in this world or the previous world you were in?" I said.

Mr Batalia hesitated for a moment deep in thought then said, "You know I can't recall. It may be just this world we are in."

"You mean we can only go so far into the future and into the past and the distance between those points is getting shorter."

"Yes. That's the way I see it," said Marco.

"And eventually those two points could meet and time will vanish," said James.

I said, "Does that mean we cease to exist?"

"Not necessarily. We may exist in some state." He replied.

Marco said, "I don't even know whether it's just concentrated here on Earth or the whole Universe is experiencing it. By that I mean no matter where you stand in the Universe you are surrounded by a contracting sphere of time."

We all thought for a moment then James said, "Looks like we have no idea. But it's quite possible it could be getting shorter in length."

"But what is causing it? Is it us with our time travelling?" I said. For I feared sometimes that we were actually the cause of all the problems we encountered.

"I don't know!" said Mr Batalia getting quite frustrated with our questions.

James replied, "OK, let's assume that it is contracting. Then we need to know how long we have before it is reduced to nothing, so to speak."

"And how will we do that?" said Mr Batalia.

After a moment's thought I realised there was only one option.

"There is only one way." I said, feeling rather fearful, "We use the time machine to see how far we can travel to the future and the past."

Mr Batalia said, "Isn't that a bit dangerous? What happens when you reach one of those end points? You might vanish, cease to exist or get stuck there."

"Does anyone have a better plan?" I said, "As far as I know we are the only people in the world with a device that can investigate this phenomenon."

James looked at me and said, "Well, I'm up for it if you are, Elizabeth."

I must be careful in future when making an argument not to find I become responsible for implementing the consequences of its conclusion.

--- ∼ ---

Chapter Seven

J.

I must make a note to allow a small-time gap between what enters my head and what comes out of my mouth. It was agreed unanimously that we were just the right people to carry out this expedition though I cannot quite remember now what the arguments were. Marco, to be fair, did volunteer, possibly because he preferred our company to Jill's.

After a little hesitation we agreed he could come, mainly because of his expertise on time engineering.

Carrying the bags that Jill had brought us, we toured the outside of the house again to retrieve the conical device which was still sitting in the courtyard in 187,. This time I had a chance to get a better idea of the interior. The walls which I had not really noticed before were a deep red and glistened, possibly a product of the exotic metals used in their construction. In the centre sat the familiar blue globe of Earth and the orange one of Mars and around each was a rotating circular brass band with a steel pointer. I went over to the Earth globe and confirmed its pointer was over the rough location of Hamgreen. For more accurate spatial positioning on the planets' surfaces beside each globe were four brass Vernier scales. I had not seen these instruments since childhood metalwork lessons where we would use Vernier callipers to measure more accurately the diameters of rods and plates. I never understood metalwork and consistently came bottom of the class - a fact which I haven't got around to mentioning to my brainbox of a wife yet

To the left, framed against the wall, were the time dials. An illuminated blue plaque beneath them displayed the current date and time. 20:00 14:10:000001873. And next to it was a similar screen in green displaying zero. Its purpose, according to Marco, was to display the time yet to elapse before arriving at the point in the past or future as set on the time dials.

So the plan was to explore the limits of time. However, the first question was: should we go to the future or past? The second was: how far do we go? And, oh yes, the third, more importantly, what do we do when we get there?

We decided to address the second first, the first second and the third when we got there. Because that's the way adventurers make decisions.

I said to Marco. "We know the Milky Way has disappeared so that gives us an upper limit of about 30,000 years either way, presuming of course, we are sitting on the centre of the finite timeline."

"I agree." He said, still looking a little uncomfortable from his decision to join us. "So, let's take it in tranches. We'll try one-hundred-year steps and watch if the star field density changes."

Elizabeth said, "I understand your logic and concur but shall we go to the future or the past?"

Marco said, "Let's toss a coin."

She said, " I prefer a task whose success is not dependent on chance. Perhaps we should go forward to the year 2016 as it is a time we know exists."

We agreed this seemed a good idea, for no other reason that good ideas seemed in short supply and Marco set the dials for that date and the blue screen changed from zero to 143 years.

"OK, let's wind up the power." He said and went over to a console to the right of the globes and after pressing a big red button, grasped a large lever protruding from a slot and carefully pushed it up. There was a slight humming sound and the pointers on a dial next to the lever slowly turned clockwise until it reached a stop bar. The wall behind the globes lit up to display a 360-degree panorama of Elizabeth's house.

"Now to change time." He said.

He touched a second lever on the console and pushed it very slowly upwards. The green time display immediately began to drop and the seasons on the wall slowly changed. Winter, snow then the green leaves of spring. I expected to see a flicker from night and day but I couldn't see it. After about ten seconds it had dropped a year and we were back in the autumn again. Seeing it was working Marco moved the lever further up and the countdown increased in speed. Within about a minute we had arrived in 2016.

I went up to the wall screen. Everything looked roughly the same and I could see plenty of stars. I said, " Looking at this all we can say is that the time line limit in the future is, er, at least 143 years. Up for a trip to the past everybody?"

---~---

E.

I was just about to agree for the voyage to the past when I had a thought. "Could you wait a minute - I think I have an idea on how to calculate where time ends."

They both stopped and looked at me. "How?" said James.

"I believe in your world, James, you know the distances to most of the stars. If we could obtain such information for a range of stars from say ten to three thousand light years we could look for those that are missing. That way we can find out roughly when time stops."

"Brilliant!" said James with more admiration for me than I was expecting. "I can use the net while we are in 2016 and get the distances of the brightest stars and nebulae."

James tapped away on his phone and tried to look up a range of stellar objects.

"Something's wrong here. Half the stars are missing. Oh, of course, in this world they don't exist as their light hasn't reached us yet. Luckily I should have an astro app from our world I can use, I hope."

James pressed some more buttons then said, "Ok, they're all here. I've got a good range including the Orion Nebula, Sirius, Aldebaran, Betelgeuse and Rigel. Marco! Move us forward to the next clear night."

We then looked at the evening sky. My favourite constellation Orion the Hunter followed by his dog rose in the eastern sky. But as I regarded its beauty I noticed something was missing. It was the central star of his belt. James noticed it too and said, "That's a bit of luck. The nebula is about 1344 lightyears and the centre star, what's it called, ah yes, Alnilan - it's 1350 light years away. Therefore, the edge is about 1344 years ago! Well done!"

I said, "If I understand you then we can't go back further than, let me see, yes, about 530 AD."

"So anything happening around that time in history?" said Mr Batalia.

"As far as I can remember we were deep in the Dark Ages here and the Saxons were taking over the country." replied James.

I said to him, "May I borrow your phone?"

I had to prise it out of his hand.

"Now, where is the mine of information again, James?"

He reluctantly pointed to a little icon on the screen and I pressed it. A white box appeared. I typed in '530 AD'.

I was quite staggered by what I found.

"There is a record that Haley's Comet appeared in 530 AD! I remember my father describing its appearance in 1835. He said there was much hysteria in the broadsheets about the end of the world but nothing came of it. Just a minute! Here is an article concerning reports in the fifth century from a person called Procopius. He says, gosh!

"'In 537 AD... this year the most dread portent took place. The sun gave forth its light without brightness, during this whole year, and it seemed like the sun in eclipse, for the beams it shed were not clear nor such as it is accustomed to shed. And from the time when this thing happened men were free neither from war nor pestilence nor any other thing leading to death.'

This is too much of a coincidence, James."

He took back his phone and read the report, "Alright. We've got a reason for the boundary at this time if this chap Procopius is to be believed. But it's only a theory. I suggest if we're going to find the edge we take it carefully. So let's get back to 1873 and start."

We arrived back in 1873, and Mr Batalia set the time to 1740. I must admit part of me was looking forward to seeing how my home changed.

The display started decreasing. As I watch us arrive at the turn of the eighteenth century I noticed the trees getting smaller and younger. Then around 1780 the house seemed to shrink in size! I quickly realised I was watching its reconstruction in reverse.

Much of the house with its ashlar walls had disappeared

and been replaced with timber frames with a single gable at the front. Only the entrance stone pillars and arched doorway of my home remained. I could now see the terracotta pantiled roof which had been hidden from view by the facade. Between the stonework and wooden joists, the wattle and daub was painted yellow. It looked very homely. When we stopped at 1740 to observe the stars again, it took some emotional resistance not to ask if I could meet my ancestors.

Mr Batalia looked at the night sky and after a few minutes in which he and James referred to their notes he said, "No obvious change in the star fields. Shame about your house, Mrs Urquhart. Right, let's try another hundred years."

We continued on our travels, stopping every hundred years for observation, until about 1060 when the woodland cleared and the even the house's wooden frames vanished leaving just a small stone building. It reminded me of the small Saxon church recently discovered wedged between some buildings in Bradford-upon-Avon near Bath and in my time was being restored to its original state.

Suddenly James shouted "Stop! Marco. Look at this."

Mr Batalia stopped the time machine and came over to us.

"This house is old. Those pillars in the porch must be Roman but look at the window mullions - they seem to be machine tooled."

"Good God! You're right. That didn't happen 'till the Victorian period. Shall we have a look?"

James immediately replied, "Not yet, Marco. Let's finish the job we came to do."

"You're right. Let's look at the stars."

Betelgeuse and Rigel had disappeared. Only the Dog Star still shone alone low in the sky. The sky was almost totally black save for a few bright stars which must have been our near neighbours. We were getting close to the edge of time.

---~---

J.

We had reached 600 AD. The countryside had been transformed from fields of corn to a devastated landscape covered with swathes of broken and fallen trees. It was as though a great tidal wave had swept across the land destroying all in its path. Not a soul was to be seen, and the night sky was now almost empty save for Sirius and Procyon. But in the midst of this destruction, Elizabeth's house stood alone and untouched. We slowed down to one year a minute. When we reached 558 AD Procyon disappeared. There was just the Dog Star shining bright above the horizon. Then at 544 AD it vanished. Marco immediately stopped the machine.

"OK, everyone we've got no guidance now. Call me a coward if you like but I'm going to reduce the steps to a day at a time."

We totally agreed.

After about half an hour when we reached 540 AD I noticed a light on the horizon.

I said, "What's that, Marco?"

"I don't know,. Let's take it slowly."

Unfortunately, as he said that he accidently moved us back a month.

"My God, what's that?"

We looked out. At first it seemed a black curtain had descended on the world and someone had drawn a pencil of light across it. Then I realised what it was. A mighty comet rising in the eastern sky. It was frighteningly large and seemed to hang stationary in the air. From the ball of the comet two long wispy tails stretched down below the horizon. I had only ever seen paintings or drawings of comets before or through a telescope which normally just showed a blurry smudge of light, but this was different. This was really different! This was a thing that frightened the life out of you. I tried to imagine what it must have been like to people used to living in a fixed small universe.

I said, "Do you think this is the cause of the time edge?"

Elizabeth said, "I do not know, James, but seeing such an apparition suddenly appear in the sky, even with the knowledge I have now, would make me think my time had come."

I replied, "Well, I think this thing is telling us we are now very close to where the end of time is. Move forward into the daytime, Marco. Let's see what we've got".

The wreckage of trees now covered an almost barren landscape, peppered with small clumps of couch grass but the house or building seemed untouched.

As we surveyed the desolate countryside Marco said, "Ok. I think this is the time to have a closer look at this building. It's just not the stonework that worries me. It's survived almost un-weathered up to the sixteenth century and occupies exactly the spot where Elizabeth's house will stand. Is that a coincidence? There's something strange about it."

--- ~ ---

E.

I must admit I was not too willing to leave the comfort of our machine but I could see if we needed to understand this adventure we had to do as he said.

We moved the machine as close to the house as we could. The sky was wild with ragged clouds racing across a weak midday sun. In the west, dark clouds were gathering lit here and there by hidden bolts of lightning. As James opened the door and we alighted on to the ground we were greeted by a blast of dusty cold air. I was glad I had changed into my Victorian clothes. Between the two Roman pillars of what seemed to be the entrance was the familiar recessed arch and wooden studded door, or so I thought, for when James touched it he said it felt like the texture of metal. At that point, expecting some unknown trickery, I hastily looked behind me and was reassured to see our time carriage was still there.

Marco said, "Shall I knock?"

We both nodded though not without some considerable nervousness on my part for my mind now held an image of a savage creature from the Dark Ages with a large axe waiting inside to murder us or worse. A moment later the door opened and we were confronted by a blank wall like that in my home of the future. But before we could say or do anything my father's head and then his body emerged like a corpse floating to the surface of a pond. I now understood why Jill screamed when she had seen James' head unexpectedly appear through the front door of my house for mine was of a similar volume.

When I has recovered I said, "Father! What are you doing here?"

"Ah! You have arrived, Lizzy. Well done. Please come in. Mr Wells is waiting for you."

---~---

Chapter Eight

J.

We followed Elizabeth's father through to what I took to be the parlour. Expecting some Dark Age open fire and straw-strewn floor I was astonished to find it had all the modern trappings of a late Victorian house complete with a stove range and a welsh dresser displaying the latest willow patterned plates. Hyatt was sitting on a battered upholstered rocking chair which looked like it had been banished from the drawing room years ago for the crime of being too comfortable and was drinking what smelt deliciously like cocoa. Wells was on a three-cornered stool by the open grate holding a thick slice of bread over the smouldering embers. Oh, and I nearly forgot, perched on the sideboard inside one of those upturned glass jars normally reserved for dead endangered species was a winged Martian. It was certainly playing the part of a stuffed creature for it was motionless. However, what was more disconcerting were its eyes which were open and looking straight at me!

I blinked. When I opened my eyes again to my surprise I found it was still there. Usually when I tried to look at them on Earth directly they vanished.

When Wells saw me he said. "Ah, Mr Urquhart. Welcome. I see you have noticed our little friend. Oh, and your good wife too. And my favourite loose cannon Mr Batalia. What year is it out there?"

I said we thought it was 540 AD.

"Then you stopped just in time, if you'll excuse the play on words. How did you know?"

I told him how we used the distance of the visible stars to

calculate the edge of time.

"Ah, the wonders of science. What would we do without it? But you must be hungry. Would you like some tea and toast? I have some nice strawberry jam fresh from my garden."

I'd forgotten how good the taste and smell of lightly toasted fresh bread were.

When we had finished, I said. "Ok. You know why we are here. What are you doing here? And what's the Martian doing in the corner?"

Wells looked at us and said, "So many questions. Please come into the drawing room. It is more comfortable for a story there although Mr Hyatt prefers this room because of that armchair."

Hyatt pretended to be hurt and replied, "But wells it is such a comfortable chair. I'm sure it could be tolerated in the drawing room."

To which Wells, resting his hand on Hyatt's shoulder, replied, rather sympathetically, "Mr Hyatt, you know, that would upset the symmetry."

And then we followed Wells down a corridor lined with pictures and etchings of what seemed to be very undressed reclining winged nymphs and shepherds with background landscapes of snow-capped mountains. I thought they didn't seem to mind the cold.

--- ~ ---

E.

I helped James along the corridor suggesting as we went that this was not the time to stop and examine the finer points of eighteenth century brush strokes and pencil lines.

When we arrived at the end of the hall I was greeted to my complete surprise with almost an exact copy of my drawing room at Hamgreen.

"Do you like it, Lizzy?" said my father. I was about to reply with a hundred questions when I noticed on the side board an exact replica of the jar with the Martian we had seen in the parlour. I wondered whether it was the same one.

"Now, please sit down," said Wells, ignoring the obvious direction of my gaze, "Are you sitting comfortably?"

We arranged ourselves as well as we could. James and I sat on a dark green sofa embroidered with game birds. Mr Batalia decided to stand by the fireplace. He did not seem relaxed in the presence of the Martian.

"Very well then," said Mr Wells. "Let me begin and try to explain what I think I have understood from our little friends. You remember the great catastrophe on Mars when the third moon crashed to the surface and destroyed the seas? Good. Unfortunately, it was not only Mars that suffered. Due to the vagaries of gravity, the orbit and pull of Jupiter, etcetera, which I could not begin to calculate, the great comet of Mr. Halley came close to Mars and interacted with the third moon. This affected the comet's orbit resulting in it coming dangerously close to our world. You may have noticed it in the sky when you arrived?"

Seeing that we all nodded though slightly open-mouthed, he continued, "When the comet first appeared in the sky, it caused the usual commotion from crackpots and charlatans heralding the end of the world. However, this time their predictions almost came true."

James said, rather too flippantly, I thought, "The firework display must have been spectacular."

"Yes, they were, Mr Urquhart. And well documented," said Wells and continued: "The consequences of this dreadful event did not occur immediately. There were many weeks during which the unfortunate souls on Earth could observe their impending doom. And when it fell to Earth it was catastrophic although luckily not as severe as that on Mars. This was of course no compensation to those who experienced it. The destruction caused sufficient damage in this part of the world to destroy the embryos of a new civilisation that was emerging."

James said, "Was this around 536 AD by any chance?"

"Exactly," said Mr Wells, "It was not the best time for such an event to occur. The Romans had left Britain over a hundred years before and due to changes in sea levels the Saxons were arriving here looking for a new home causing much conflict with the Britons. They were a rather primitive race in the eyes of the those who had lived with, or remembered, the Roman world but although they did not use stone they were fine carpenters and metalworkers. I'm sure you have seen their handiwork in museums. There had been some effort for the two races to accommodate each other but the arrival of the fragments from Mars, which are recorded in the literature as fiery comets, destroyed any hope of unity."

"And so the real Dark Ages in Britain began," said Mr Batalia.

"Yes." said Mr Wells.

I had listened to this with great interest as I understood this was the time of King Arthur who had become very fashionable in my father's time. He had taken me as a child to the House of Lords and the Queen's Chamber where displayed on the walls were illustrations of tales of King

Arthur from Mallory's book. I must admit I didn't completely share his enthusiasm. I had read Lord Tennyson's great poem on the Idylls of a King but found it a little too dull and flowery. James had great enthusiasm for all Victorian Arthuriana but possibly because I had grown up surrounded by it, like all generations, I preferred a fashion of a more distant past. For me the baroque was the place and time of choice.

However, when I mentioned King Arthur to Mr Wells he was quite adamant that he did not exist. He had met a certain Ambrosius Aurelius less than a year before here in the sixth century who, when he discovered his exploits had been attributed to Arthur, who according to Mr Wells was an invention of a certain Geoffrey Arthur of Monmouth in the twelfth century, was apparently very much upset.

$$--- \sim ---$$

J.

Although Wells' story filled in a few holes he had not answered the real question. I thanked him for the information then said, "So why does time stop at this catastrophe which I understand was only about four years ago from now."

He said, "I'm not sure, Mr Urquhart. I was waiting for you to find out."

"Oh thanks. No pressure then," I said and wondering whether I was carrying a large cone on my head inscribed with a big letter 'D'. "But first can you tell me how you got here and what is this place?"

"This place is a kind of stasis in time. If you could go back far enough to the Bronze Age you would find this was a burial mound with a portal to Mars. It was one of the first places on Earth the Martians visited. It is rather special because it allows movement through time but as a consequence it generated eddies or whirlpools of time. You inadvertently discovered one at the Cricket Club which led to you to your future wife."

"You didn't plan that, did you, Wells?"

"No. That was all your own work."

In this current situation I wasn't quite sure whether to be gratified or not.

"So what is this place?"

"It is my house. It survives and remains untouched because it stretches through time from its construction in the fourth century. And before you ask why it was constructed, the local Romans built it to hide the pagan burial mound."

Elizabeth said, "Then if this is your house how did my family arrive here?"

At this point her father joined the conversation.

"You remember I said my good friend Mr William Dawes had given me a map of the canals of Mars, James?"

I remembered it well and the three or four glasses of whiskey that went with it. "Yes, it was a pleasant evening."

"And you also remember that sometimes late at night William and I, on our walks back from the Lammastide, had seen the Martians?"

At this point Elizabeth interrupted. "Father! You used to tell me that you and Mr Dawes were at Chilbury at a Bridge Club. Instead while I was looking after Flory I discover you were out supping ale!"

"But, Lizzy, you were such a good baby sitter and I so enjoyed your hot chocolate when I returned."

I squeezed Elizabeth 's hand because we needed to get his story.

He noticed and giving her a father's sympathetic smile continued. "What I hadn't said was how long we had been seeing them. They had been around us, Lizzy, for a long time. So long in fact they were known to your grandfather. They are the reason why we live at Hamgreen."

Little by little, questions unanswered and questions unasked began to fall into place.

"Your grandfather, Lizzy, was quite a lively character. I wish you had met him. Unfortunately, he died before you were born. You would have liked him. He was a gentle and tolerant man who had managed, despite a rather varied life style, to reach the grand old age of eighty. However, in his younger years, just after the turn of the century, he was well known in Bath Society which I'm sure you can imagine required a certain expenditure. Unfortunately, it was not an expenditure commensurate with his incomes despite his success in investing in some of the grander squares and crescents. But I digress again. One day while walking home from a rather late soiree at his Club across the Pulteney Bridge he noticed strange lights in one of the shops. Hs curiosity took the better of him."

He stopped and turned to Elizabeth and said with a grin. "You see, Lizzy, it runs in the family."

He then continued. "He opened the shop door which rang a bell. At first he saw no one for he found he was distracted by a most peculiar room full of what he thought were strange nautical devices. But then he noticed behind a bench a gentleman in unusual costume studying a map. On seeing my father, he stood and shaking his hand said, 'Good Evening Mr Bicester, I hoped you would drop in. My father assures me they were the exact words!"

I looked at Wells who was feigning complete disinterest with his feet up on a cushion looking at the Martian. I said to him, "And I presume that was you, Wells. You do get around, don't you? How many shops have you got?" for I remembered I'd met him in such a shop in Charing Cross the year before I met Elizabeth.

Wells pretended to ignore my remark and continued to look at the Martian while Elizabeth's father continued: "He said he had a proposition for him. My father who at that time was a little concerned with the direction in which his money was flowing and possibly had taken more drink than was sensible for a young man listened with interest.

"It was a simple proposition. The gentleman wished my father to have a house in Sussex where he and his family could live gratuitously for as long as they wished providing they would accommodate certain visitors from time to time. My father, possibly aided by the evening's wine and port, saw this as an opportunity not to be missed and agreed, on the provision that he saw the place first. A week later he was safely ensconced here and found as a consequence the river on which his monies was sailing away had come to halt. So there you are."

"And I presume these visitors included creatures like the one in that jar over there?" I said.

"Exactly, Mr Urquhart. They have been no trouble at all. They just come and go."

"Except now and again you experience inexplicable time shifts."

"Of course. My father and I have seen many places and times."

--- ~ ---

E.

I could not believe what I was hearing!

I said, "Father, forgive me, but I must speak my mind. This is too much! All that time I was left on my own you were buffeting about up and down the centuries, I suppose you were in cahoots with Mr Wells in manipulating James as well?"

"Of course I did. Do you not think he is a good match for you?"

I looked at James who had a rather stunned expression upon his face. "Please do not tell me you are complicit in this charade as well?"

"Certainly not, Elizabeth! I am quite shocked being used like this."

At this point, Mr Wells, who until that moment had expressed no interest in this exchange said, "I can assure you that both of you have not been used. A trail of clues and hooks had been set for some years. Many people found them but only you two had the curiosity and free minds to pick them up and understand them. You should congratulate yourself and also have some sympathy for your father who could only stand aside and watch. You do not know how much he loves you, Mrs Urquhart."

I looked at my father. He was twiddling his thumbs and had that comforting smile I remembered he reserved for me when I was young and found myself vulnerable in a world I did not understand. I was about to reach out and embrace him when Wells said, "Now, as we are all here, we must address the real task: the end of time."

As he said it I noticed the room had become quite dark. Without prompting Mr Hyatt stood up and said he would fetch candles. A weak light cast shadows on the walls, removing much of the colour. I went to the window and to my amazement saw the tree-lined courtyard as it stood in my time silhouetted by an evening sky fleeced with golden clouds. I turned to Mr Wells for an explanation.

"What time is it here, Mr Wells?"

"In here it is always 1895. But for you it is time to go."

James said, "And what are we expected to do?"

"That is your choice. You can explore the end of time or you can go back home. There are no constraints."

--- ~ ---

Chapter Nine

J.

No constraints indeed! Wells knew our natural curiosity would get the better of us.

We stepped through the portal door of the house and saw again the great comet floating in the sky just above the glowing horizon. It was unnatural, like a death white nebulous head with its two shrouds trailing behind. In the west a red-horned moon and Mars added to the hellish landscape which I'm sure Dante could have used in his first book. The air smelt of burnt hay.

It was just Elizabeth and me who formed the heroic team as Marco had decided it was best to 'volunteer' to stay behind, ready, as he explained it, to help out if or when we returned. Though what help that would be forthcoming.

I opened the door of the machine and we entered. The sound of the wind abating gave us a semblance of protection.

"Which way shall we go, Elizabeth?"

"You know there is only one way."

I really must find a girl who runs away at the first sign of adversity so I don't have to pretend to be the hero.

I pushed the time lever gently towards 536 AD. At first nothing seemed to happen. The wild scene on the wall didn't change but as we got closer to what we thought was the time edge a shower of molten, glowing rocks suddenly lifted up to the sky from the horizon and became meteorites which travelled towards the comet. We sped backwards through days and watched more and more glowing fragments as they rose up to the sky. On the horizon the air flickered in hues of red and orange. I could not imagine what hell it was for those witnessing it in the sixth century while we sat safely, or we hoped safely, inside the machine. Suddenly the broken trees around us rose and righted themselves although they were affected by storm filled winds which blew towards the north. Then an orange, glowing, elongated ball flew up into the sky no more than half a mile away. As we watched its fiery trail a shadow appeared on the horizon and grew bigger. At first we didn't comprehend what was going on until to our horror we realised it was a wall of earth rising like a wave and coming towards us!

We held each other tight frozen with fear. The wall rose higher and higher. Then my nerve broke and I reached for the time lever to propel us back to our future. But just at that exact moment the vision changed. I still do not know whether I, or time, changed it but we found ourselves on Mars. A Mars of blue skies and oceans.

--- ~ ---

E.

I was transfixed by the suddenness of the apparition before me. My mind was still racing from the shock of being plucked from what I thought were the jaws of death. I was standing on a golden shore. Before me great blue waves slowly rose and fell in the weak gravity. I recognised where we were but it was impossible! In the sky hung Phobos and Deimos. But then I realised 'when' we were for the third moon appeared over the horizon and once again Marco's white boat appeared sliding up and down the waves towards us.

James grabbed my hand, "We're here again! And there's Marco coming towards us. How did we come back here?"

"Move the date forward quick!" I shouted for I feared we would find ourselves travelling in some circle of time around the nexus from which we could not escape. James pushed the lever forward. With relief we found we were still on Mars but as we moved into the Martian future, to our horror the moon started to fall toward us.

I realised my mistake almost too late, "It's the wrong way, James! We have to go back to the nexus!"

"What? God, you're right!"

He pulled back the lever and the moon receded. Then we arrived at the nexus and found ourselves back on Earth only to be confronted with the mountainous wall or wave of earth rising towards us again! Without prompting James moved us forward in time and thankfully the wall receded, the trees fell back to the ground, and we found ourselves outside the house again in relative calm.

"Oh, I'm so sorry, James, I did not think," I said.

"But you did think and I thought it was the right move as well 'till it was bloody obvious to both of us it wasn't."

"Yes. But I wish, if you do not mind me taking a liberty with your language, James, I wish sometimes that things were more 'bloody' obvious a little sooner. I do not know how we get away with it sometimes."

"Nor do I. But now I've got a great idea."

"I'm not convinced I can take any more ideas."

"It's simple. We just sneak off to the future together and leave them all to it in that cursed house."

A sudden warmth of a childhood world protected from all danger washed over me. "It is an idea with great merit." I replied, "We will throw this confounded machine into the sea, then go home, change the locks, hide under the stairs and answer the door to no one."

"Yes, and we will only come out to make cake and babies."

I came close to him. I felt our hearts beating still fast and I whispered, "James, you should know that I would not normally accept that latter proposition in a place like this without due consideration but," I gently bit his ear, "at this moment I confess I find it singularly attractive."

"Excellent. You will be held to that when we get home. But in the meantime, shall we go and see what your damn father is up to?"

On this occasion I allowed James licence with regard to his description of my earthly creator.

--- ~ ---

J.

Marco looked as though he was quite surprised to see us when he poked his head through the portal of the house.

An image from a fairground came to my mind and I said, "Marco, have you ever thought of finding employment in a coconut shy?"

It was quite gratifying to see the confusing look on his face not helped by Elizabeth 's rather unladylike snort of laughter.

We went through the portal into the warm safety of the house. Hyatt, Wells and Elizabeth's father were in the drawing room sitting around a table covered in drawings and maps. I could see her father was visibly moved by her safe return for he embraced her very enthusiastically for a Victorian.

Wells came over and shook my hand and said, "Well done

on returning, now please sit down and tell us what you saw if you can. But first I imagine you may be hungry."

He turned to Hyatt and said, "Mr Hyatt, would you be good enough to make our intrepid adventurers some tea? There is some bread pudding in the larder which I'm sure Mr Urquhart will appreciate."

Hyatt got up from the table, congratulated us on our return and shook my hand. And then being not sure how to greet Elizabeth shook her hand as well before disappearing into the parlour.

When we had finished recounting our trip, Wells pondered for a minute or so while we listened to the whistle of the kettle getting louder in the kitchen. When it stopped, accompanied by a muffled cry from Hyatt regarding the surprising conductive properties of metal pots, Wells said, "So what you saw suggests to me the catastrophe on Mars and Earth must be linked in time."

I agreed, "Yes, it's too much of coincidence. As we hit the time barrier we popped up on Mars just in time to witness its destruction."

Elizabeth said, "Yes, but what was unaccountable was that we arrived at exactly that time at, which we saw Mr Batalia in his boat."

Marco said, "What? You saw me? So why didn't you wait for me?"

"Because," I answered, "We feared we would find ourselves repeating that adventure all over again."

"So you just left me with the world about to end!"

"Yep. No, I'm only kidding, Marco. I'm sure the Marco that we saw will meet us in that timeline, if you get what I mean, and rescue you. Otherwise, we wouldn't be having this conversation."

Before Marco could respond Wells brought us back to the subject. "Thank you, Mrs Urquhart. This must be a clue. It indicates that somehow time can be bent."

There was then another silence which was thankfully interrupted by Hyatt bringing in a tray of tea and cake. We tucked in. While contemplating whether to grab the last piece of bread pudding or offer it to Elizabeth an idea came to me. I said, "I think time has been distorted or fractured."

I looked around the table. No encouragement, only expectation, so I carried on. "Let me show you. Give me some paper from that table and a pen or pencil."

I drew a number of parallel lines on a piece of paper.

"Imagine," I said, holding up the paper, "this paper is Space and these are alternative time lines stretching from the past to the future through it. We know we can somehow cross from one time line to another but up to now I didn't think they crossed. Now watch."

I then tore the paper into two strips, then put them back together again on the table.

"See the lines are continuous across the strips, but if I move one of the strips sideways the lines are broken. All time is still here but it is disjointed and so you cannot travel from here to here."

Wells said, "So what you are saying is that all of history is still here, but we can't reach it anymore?"

"It's only a theory. But watch this." I said, moving one of the strips at right angles to the timelines. "You see if you move this strip here further sideways the lines join up again."

"Of course. They are now joined to different timelines!" exclaimed Wells. "So, if you go past this tear or fracture you end up in a different timeline."

"Very clever, Urquhart," said Marco. "But that doesn't explain how you arrived on Mars?"

"I can only think that not only is time fractured but space as well. However, to visualise and understand that you need to see in five dimensions."

At that point everyone turned to the Martian who was now looking straight at me.

--- ~ ---

E.

The Martian creature, which had sat on the corner table under its glass cover almost unnoticed, was changing colour. Its white skin, if that was what it was, was now rippling with hues of the rainbow. Small gossamer wings lifted slowly from its back and fluttered minutely like a hummingbird. Then it turned its gaze towards me. I grabbed James' arm with both hands as I felt that familiar dream-like sleep waft over me. Once again, a fear thrilled through me but I felt James' hand touch mine and I was not afraid.

The room dissolved and I was far away in space, black space, looking down on the planets. Shadows flickered close by. Then imperceptibly at first the worlds and moons slowly elongated into tubes of colour. They grew longer and longer and as they stretched out into space they twisted into corkscrew spirals which followed a path around the sun which itself was growing into a yellow orange glowing rod. It was beautiful. And then its wonder came to me. I realised I was seeing as a Martian saw our world. I was seeing time!

As they twisted around the sun's path a white line suddenly appeared growing brighter and brighter which curved towards the Earth. But before I could look closer the whole vision became distorted by an invisible wave which pushed the tubes and lines backwards and forwards. Then another ripple, then another but each less powerful than before. It reminded me of being at the seaside amongst the rock pools where the ebb and flow of the waves tossed the seaweed and starfish back and forth.

Then the scene faded, and I found myself back in the drawing room.

I turned to James, his hand still holding mine tight but before I could speak Marco said. "Did you all see what I just saw?"

We nodded silently.

"Thank God for that!" He exclaimed with some relief. "I'd thought you'd drugged me with the tea."

I ignored his rather crude remark and the disappointment of not thinking of doing that to him a long time ago for I had noticed the Martian had returned to its white immobile self.

--- ~ ---

J.

I'd guessed since we saw that Martian perched on the gatepost on our visit to Hamgreen that they had an interest in what we were doing although until now it hadn't been clear what they were up to nor why they had waited till now to help. But maybe they'd been helping us all along in their own way. What was obvious though was they seemed to need our help. But for what? As far as I could tell this Martian had tried to show us what had happened by trying to present his five dimensional universe in our 3D world. But why did it need to tell us? Were we expected to deduce something from our group dream and carry out some action?

I thought I'd ask Wells first.

He said. "My view is they have shown the passage of our solar system through time by making time look like a spatial dimension. But I do not subscribe to that view. Time is time"

"Yes, Wells, but we all move through space-time at the speed of light which suggests it has spatial properties."

"But we are here, and I don't feel us moving at all."

"That's because we only see in 3D. We are travelling actually through time at the speed of light even when we are standing still. Everything - and I mean everything - is travelling at the speed of light. Not a bit less or a bit more. That was Einstein 's great insight."

"But when I drive or ride I would then go faster than that speed."

"No. Time slows down or space contracts so that you still travel at light speed. In the four dimensional world of space-time everything travels at that speed."

"But when a light beam travels, what happens to time?" said Mr Hyatt demonstrating he was obviously doing a good job at keeping up.

"It's reduced to zero." I said, "A light beam takes no time to go from point to another."

"That cannot be right for we know that light from the nearest star takes about four years to reach us."

"Yes. That is because its distance in space is four light years and we travel along our timeline for four years and to us that's the time it takes. But if you sat on the light beam you would arrive here in no time at all."

Hyatt said, "Sorry, Mr Urquhart, I have lost the road

now."

Elizabeth said, ignoring Hyatt. "But what about those ripples which buffeted the moons and planets? Did you see them, James?"

"Yes, I did. I think what we were watching was a massive gravitational wave from a collapsing star or galaxy."

There was then much discussion where I tried quite abysmally to explain the concepts of black holes, super novae and how space could be squeezed and stretched.

When Elizabeth began to realise I was on the limits of my knowledge and about to topple off she came to my rescue. Just in time, I might add, as even I was beginning to not believe what I was saying.

"So if I understand correctly," she said holding my hand again for she could see I was getting a little stressed with being the house answering service, "this wave buffets space, wobbling everything about and causing the moon to crash on Mars and send Halley's comet closer to Earth."

"Yes." I said, relieved that someone was following me. "And when we reach 536 AD we hit this wobble which is so powerful it makes it impossible to travel further back in time."

"I thought the Martians tried to destroy the moon but failed to do it properly," said Marco.

"Maybe they would have done it properly if the gravitational wave hadn't passed through the solar system." I said.

"Point taken."

"But why do you end up on Mars?" said Wells.

"And Urquhart," said Marco, throwing in another penny's worth. "Why is it we used to be able to see the Milky Way and can't see it now?"

I was beginning to understand what it must have been like to be Chief Wizard in a primitive village. Everyone keeps on asking you questions you can't answer or they can't be bothered to answer themselves. And the more questions you answer the more they ask. Eventually the people stop thinking for themselves and the wise wizard gives up as well and just feeds them anything that comes into his head.

I'm sure one of the big problems with our species is if something seems sensible, we believe it's right. You know what I mean. From my seat here the earth is flat and the Sun goes around the Earth. Obvious to anyone who looks, isn't it? Then some bright spark asks what's holding the flat earth up and you tell then it's sitting on a turtle, hoping they'll go away. Then another hundred years goes by with everyone happy with that until some idiot asks what's the turtle sitting on? Eventually you have to tell them you made it up and it's all lies and actually the Earth is round and goes around the Sun. This goes down well because they tell you they've always thought the Sun God was really important and it makes sense he should be at the centre of the universe. However, when you tell them, a bit too smugly, it's just one of billions of suns and we live in a dark nondescript place on the edge of a galaxy and they should all grow up and live with it, they begin to doubt your wisdom. Then just when you're consoling yourself that you're the only intelligent person in the village and everyone else is a fool, some railway clerk arrives and tells the villagers that time isn't constant and solid matter is nearly all empty space even though you can't see through it. You know at that point that your wizard accolade is about to come to a sticky end. However, sensing I still had the pointy hat I continued.

"To answer your question on why we can't see the Milky

Way I think it's because somehow this ripple of gravity also shut off or absorbed all the light in its path. It must have been gigantic if it reached out as far as the Andromeda galaxy."

"So, at the event that is why the sky is black," said Elizabeth

"Yes. And as we come forward in time the light from the stars begins to arrive again. It's just that in 2016 most of the light from the stars in the Milky Way have not reached us yet."

"Seems plausible, Urquhart," said Marco.

See what I mean? If it sounds sensible then it must be true. I was just beginning to wonder where I could introduce the turtle into my explanation when Elizabeth, sensing I was beginning to lose my marbles, came to my assistance.

--- ∼ ---

E.

I felt that it was a little unfair that James and I were having to answer all the questions as we had not volunteered for anything and that Mr Wells, Mr Batalia and the Martian creature should be a little more accountable. It was time to bat back the balls that they were bowling at us.

"Mr Wells. What is the relationship between you and the Martians?"

For the first time in our acquaintance, he looked uncomfortable.

He said, "Have you read my manuscript on the visit of the angel?"

I replied that I had not as his books were after my time.

"It describes a creature that was thought to be one who

came to Earth and was shot by a vicar. Yes, I know. It is quite shocking. But it is a true story. I found the 'Angel' and took it under my wing so to speak. I nursed it back to health. In return it told me everything about Mars including how they could see a little into the future."

"And they showed you how to travel in time?"

"No, but they allowed me in my dreams to detach myself from my corporeal body and see the future."

"So how did you visit Mr Hyatt in your youth?"

"I took Mr Batalia's time machine."

"What!" said Mr Batalia, looking rather shocked. "When?"

"Shortly before Mr and Mrs Urquhart found me in the cavern examining the machine, I had already borrowed it for the purpose you state."

James exclaimed almost in despair, "Is there anyone here who hasn't used us?"

Mr Hyatt raised his hand in the manner of a child at his school. "I assure you I am not only innocent of participating in this adventure, but I have also little understanding of what you are all talking about."

"Thank you, Mr Hyatt." I said." You have my sympathy. Now, Mr Batalia, would you like to attempt to answer the question you posed to my husband?"

"What? How you ended up on Mars?"

"Yes. And if I you could sprinkle it with some veracity, James and I would be very grateful."

"Very well. This is what I think. Urquhart is on the right track. The gravitational ripple distorted space-time to such a degree that the space-time continuum for Mars and Earth momentarily joined. This caused the time lines to join rather like the U tube. You go back to 536 AD on Earth and you swing around the bend to Mars. Similarly, if you're on Mars, if you go back to the catastrophe there you swing around to the one on Earth."

James joined in again. "So, at the event, time looks like this."

He then retrieved a piece of paper and drew a large U and wrote Mars above one upright of the letter U and Earth above the other. He then drew a horizontal line under it with a label 536 AD. "This is what you're saying for the world we can see?"

"Yes that's right."

"Now," said James, who I was glad to see had re-found his enthusiasm for explanation again, said, "If I draw another U like this."

He drew an inverted U underneath of the same size as the other. "Then this represents time before the event."

"Exactly." said Mr Batalia. "The time before the catastrophe is separated from us. Though I don't know whether the two timelines are joined in a U like that or still separated."

I now at last had a little more comprehension of this pan-dimensional world and asked, ""So does that mean the history before the event does not reach this world?"

"But it must," said James, "Otherwise the people who survived in the sixth century would not be as advanced as they are."

"You're right, Urquhart. They haven't started from scratch. They know metal technologies and are wearing clothes."

"So those who survived brought their histories or past memories with them across the break." I said.

Mr Wells I noticed was now standing and pondering something. He looked at the sleeping Martian in the glass jar then at us. "Yes. That is the conundrum. The people here can remember the past but apparently, we cannot travel back in time past the event. What does that mean for us?"

"Nothing, really," said James, "This world has survived into the future relatively ok and the only thing that is different is as this world goes farther into the future the more stars and galaxies they will see. Personally, I'd leave everything alone and go home."

This was comfortable logic. But there was still the Martian sitting in the corner. If there was nothing to do, then why was it here? Unfortunately, when I broached this to everyone, James decided to do one of his inexplicable actions whose consequences only later in hindsight am I normally able understand and forgive.

--- ~ ---

Chapter Ten

J.

Sometimes Elizabeth makes a suggestion which at the time seems of little significance until I decide to explore it.

Although it would be nice to go home the presence of the Martian had created a nagging doubt in my mind that something was unfinished.

It was the inability to cross the time-event that was causing me the problem. I just couldn't let it go. But to cross the barrier and possibly join the past to the future we needed to see in higher dimensions. This was where the Martian came in. I felt that if I could communicate with it somehow I might get somewhere. I decided to go over to it and lift it out of the glass jar.

As I approached the jar I remembered at Helmsley how light and fragile they were. And how they slowly floated up to the sky assisted by my boot as though gravity did not affect them. Unfortunately, as I touched the jar the creature shimmered and vanished.

I turned around, noticed the rather shocked faces on the remainder of my audience and attempted, rather stupidly, to shrug my action off. "Oh well, it looks like I've managed to lose the only way out of this dilemma. Might as well go home."

This had no effect on my audience who remained stunned for what seemed a minute

Wells was the first to speak. "If you are wondering where it has gone, I think you will find it is in the time machine waiting for you."

I didn't like the sound of that 'you' bit. Nor, looking at

Elizabeth, did she. That was going to be our only route out of here and back to home. How did Wells know where it was? Was he in constant communication with them? And if so, how?

I tried rather weakly to get out of him what I knew was coming. "Come on, Wells. This isn't fair! We seem to be the only ones here doing all the work here and taking all the risks. We only just got back from the edge by a stroke of luck."

"Unfortunately," he said, "It only wants to talk with you two."

"And why is that?" I said trying to control my voice.

"Because only you two and your sister can travel through time unaided by any device."

"What do you mean, only us? ..." I searched back in my mind right back to when I had first met Elizabeth. I suddenly realised everyone else had travelled back and forth in time only by the aid of machines or portals, including Marco. Even Wells had said his corporeal self was stuck in his own present. Once again, we found ourselves in a situation where there was no escape.

"So now I've got a pet Martian waiting to take us on a journey which no one else can do?"

Wells gave a sympathetic though not reassuring nod.

What a nightmare!

Elizabeth added to my woes by saying rather crossly to me. "God, James! If only you had not touched that jar. We could have jumped into the time machine and flown safely back to our home. Now instead it is in there waiting for us with God knows what plans to entertain us!"

There was another moment of silence while I did my best to avoided Elizabeth's gaze.

Then she said, rather loudly to make sure we understood her annoyance "Right. Obviously by your silence there is no other choice so I am going to change my clothes. I am not going to have another expensive dress ruined by James dragging me through another hedge backwards."

And with that she stormed out of the room. There was rather an embarrassed silence for about ten minutes in the room as everybody tried to pretend nothing untoward had happened and ignored the sound of loud footsteps, banging of drawers and cupboards accompanied by almost inaudible mutterings emanating from the ceiling above. Eventually she returned with a carpet bag and wearing tight leggings, walking boots, a half-buttoned shirt and a suede dark brown jacket fitted with enough pockets to keep a poacher happy. I don't know what bra she was wearing but I made a mental note to buy her another half dozen at the earliest opportunity when normal relationships were restored, which I hoped would be not too far in the distant future.

However, I digress, as the effect on the Victorians was worth recording, especially Hyatt who had gone rather pink and was having difficulty keeping his eyes off her chest and bottom. Mind you I couldn't blame him. She did look good if you ignored the rather unsympathetic expression on her face. Her father, however, could not resist intervening and said in a rather unconvincing voice that comes from having two daughters who normally win an argument, "I cannot really allow you to go out dressed like that, Lizzy."

"I think after your treatment of me, Father, I think I will wear what I wish! And will you kindly address me as Elizabeth!" Ouch! Then just as I thought I might be off the hook she turned to me, grabbed my hand quite roughly and said, "Come on then, Captain Dunderhead. Let us go and see what porridge you have landed us in this time."

And with that I was dragged out of the door.

--- ~ ---

E.

We entered the accursed machine again in an uncomfortable silence after not a little discussion on the difference between suggestions and consequential actions. However, we were quickly distracted from our contemplation of James' weaknesses when we discovered, sitting on the Mars globe, the creature. As we stood there wondering what to do, and also speculating who would speak first, I heard a noise behind us and on sharply turning, observed the door closing and locking by itself. I now had that distinct feeling of one who boards the wrong train and only finds out when it starts to move out of the station.

I involuntarily moved closer to James and felt his hand reaching for mine. I have to admit despite our quarrel I only momentarily resisted his offer.

The Martian, no doubt sensing we were now safely ensconced, or trapped, inside the machine awoke and changing its hue, unfurled its gossamer wings. As they began to vibrate we and the room became strangely blurred and our bodies seemed to spread into rainbows of ghostly form. The colours slowly extended to fill the room and I realised that we were seeing ourselves as the Martians did: outside time and stretching into the past and future. I turned to James. He looked almost transparent for I could see his body through his clothes. I knew I would appear the same to him but it did not worry me for I had become immersed in this beautiful detachment from the material world. But just as I had succumbed to its fascination we suddenly rose up into the air, or more precisely up into space! We held each other tightly; all thought of that little altercation forgotten as we sought comfort in each other.

When I opened my eyes, I found we were floating or flying above the planets. I could see Halley's comet just beyond Mars with its long tale stretching towards the Sun. And everywhere a backdrop of stars. Then something even more incredible happened. Those planetary spheres which floated suspended in space began first to elongate and then extrude into twisting corkscrew rods. As I watched the beautiful intricate tubes snake around the Sun, I suddenly realised that I was seeing the paths of the planets as they passed through time from the past to the future. But then I noticed stars disappearing. It reminded me of a moonless star-bright night when invisible clouds rise above the horizon and unexpectedly hide the starlight. As I watched more and more stars disappeared. It was like a black phantom shroud which enveloped the starry firmament. I sensed its invisible cloak coming closer and closer until it rippled quietly and slowly through the ever lengthening tubes of the planets distorting their paths into almost impossible shapes. Suddenly a dark wave of this black sea caused the winding space-time rods of Mars and Earth to push together until they were almost touching and bounced back. Halley's comet, had now changed its path and was heading toward Mars! Just as I thought they were going to crash into each other, the scene froze as though someone had stopped a film in mid-motion. For a moment nothing happened then the twirling rods slowly contracted to their end points until they became spherical planets again and Mars and the comet hung impossibly close, frozen in time.

___ ~ ___

J.

The softness of her almost transparent body pressed against me, coupled with the aroma of my favourite perfume which I'm sure she must have purposely put on before coming downstairs to give me stick, caused some distraction from the vision before me. What I saw generally confirmed what we had deduced about the event. But it still didn't give me a clue as to why the Martian wanted us. As if to answer my thoughts the creature reached down to the Martian globe and moved the pointer across the surface. We literally catapulted from our little viewpoint in space to back inside the machine. The wall screens lit up and we watched us fall down to Mars to the Marina Valley. I felt my stomach leaving me behind. But as we approached the valley, unlike our last visit, where it was a dry deep chasm, now it was a torrent of churning flowing water. Except incredibly it was frozen in time! It was like a 3D photograph in which we could pass through! Then before we could catch our breaths we were racing across waves and spray held in suspended animation and up the valley towards the Tharsis volcanoes. What was really scary was above us. It was Halley's Comet, its great tails, jagged and broken, stretching across the sky. It couldn't have been more than a hundred miles away.

We came out of the head of the valley on to the Tharsis Plain. Being used to the distant horizons of Earth my mind couldn't handle the nearness of the Martian horizon, behind which slowly rose the great shield volcano of Olympus. It was impossibly huge. I had read somewhere it was about fifteen miles high and twice the area of England but from where we sat it looked as big as the planet

Then just as we approached the Arsia Volcano the machine took a steep dive into a gaping hole. Elizabeth screamed and I possibly increased though not necessarily improved her vocabulary with my contribution. The accelerations and decelerations should have squashed us flat like strawberry jam against the walls half a dozen times but we felt nothing. We continued our descent down a tunnel until we emerged into a gigantic cavern. Its floor rushed up to us but just as I thought we were going to smash into the ground we stopped in an instant a few feet above the surface and the screen went blank.

As we stood there exhausted from the ride I noticed the machine was now quiet. In fact, there was not a sound except our breathing. According to the time on the blue display it was 536 AD. We were at the time fracture.

We waited what seemed ages for something else to happen, but nothing did, just a quiet room with a Martian who had now returned to its normal colourless stone-like appearance.

After a while Elizabeth withdrew her arms from me and whispered. "So what do we do now? I presume we are not going to implement any of those extraordinary suggestions you made during the descent."

I was a bit reticent to say anything after our recent conversations but carried on anyway.

"I'm afraid Captain Conker Head hasn't got a clue."

"It is Dunderhead. Do you not listen to anything I say?"

"Obviously only your suggestions."

"Then I will endeavour to keep them to myself in future."

Silence again accompanied by the withdrawal of her body.

After a further moment she said, "Very well., on this occasion I will make allowances for your actions if you take up my suggestion to open the door."

I decided to act rather than reply, for I have found from experience that a woman should always have the last word in an argument, for if the man has the last word, it usually results in the start of a new argument. I reached for the door but to my surprise it opened by itself. We looked at each other and still saying nothing to ensure compliance with my rule, I shrugged my shoulders resignedly and went through the opening. Elizabeth, I was glad to see followed close behind.

The cavern was lit by an orange luminous glow which seemed to emanate from the walls and floor. They were incredibly smooth and featureless as though they had been coated with plastic. Up above, far above, there was a circular opening to a dark sky. The place was completely empty if you discounted the sleek cobalt blue Martian spaceship hovering motionlessly in the centre. It was long and smooth with four fin-like wings. It reminded me of one of those spaceships you find on the cover of a 1950s SF magazine. It was usually accompanied by a square-jawed hero and his rather pneumatically inflated girlfriend who, judging by their enthusiastic expressions, were ready to take on the universe. Unfortunately, try as I might I could not see anybody fitting their description anywhere in the cavern.

--- ~ ---

E.

It was obvious that the beautiful blue rocket was waiting to transport James and me to a new unknown. Not least because as we alighted from the time machine its door closed behind us with a loud disconcerting click.

Despite my first thought on hearing that sound to attempt to return to its safety, I decided that this was not quite the right time to ask James if he had a key to the door's lock as I knew the reply would possibly undo any advantage I had gained from our previous discussions.

Instead, I asked, "Shall we try to find the door to this rocket?" For I could see no other exit from our predicament. But before James could respond a hatch opened at the side from which descended a small ladder. He looked at me with an expression indicating that he had had more than sufficient admonishment for one day and said, "Any other suggestions before we enter?"

I took his hand, "No, James."

With one last look around to see if there was any evidence of a reprieve from our situation I ascended the ladder as closely behind him as possible for I did not want to discover the vehicle was designed for just one idiot.

--- ~ ---

J.

We emerged in an oval, blue-lit room. There were two couches each with its own control panel complete with steering wheels. Someone or something had obviously gone to some effort to design this cockpit for human comfort. The walls of the room, which were of a bronze metallic colour were smooth and blank.

Seeing nothing else to do, such as run away, because the hatch from which we had entered had just closed with an un-reassuring hiss behind us, we decided without suggestion to carefully sit on the two couches. However, as we tried to make ourselves comfortable, they immediately changed shape to not only accommodate our bodies but to envelop them. We were now trapped and, I realised, drawing a little comfort from it, we were possibly in the best crash seats that had ever been invented. Then to reinforce what both of us were expecting next, the two steering wheels and consoles moved towards us until they were comfortably in reach of our hands.

Elizabeth was the first to speak. "James?"

"Yes?"

"Although I know you admire my dog cart driving and I have extricated us from one or two tight corners which you had not expected, I have to tell you that I have never driven a vehicle with a steering wheel. When you turn it clockwise does a vehicle turn to my left or the other left?"

"Usually turning it clockwise turns the vehicle right."

"But I have been on a steam launch with such a thing and found turning it clockwise caused it to turn left. Perhaps I should try it?"

Before I could stop her she turned the wheel clockwise a little and all hell broke loose. The walls of the cockpit lit up to show the outside cavern and flashing horizontal bands of green and red lights appeared on the console. Oh, and the entire cavern started slowly rotating to the left.

"Let go of the wheel!"

The cavern motion came to a halt and the lights dimmed on the console. I was gratified to see it had a self-centring mechanism.

"My God, James! What have I done?"

"You've followed your own suggestion."

I thought I might have overplayed that one but when she

looked at me still with shock on her face she said, "What an idiot I am in this sea of madness! I am not fit to be let out. What a pair we are! Surely there is someone out there that could do a better job than us?"

"Well, if there is, he's obviously seen what we're up against and kept himself well hidden."

"All I can say is if I find him, he will be severely admonished for allowing us to suffer so."

"But just think what he's missing."

"What could possibly want him to share this adventure?"

"Being with you of course."

A smile at last. She tried to struggle out of the couch. "Oh, this damn thing," she said, "Now I can't even kiss you!"

--- ～ ---

E.

I was trapped in a cocoon far in the past in a strange device of Martian making inside a cavern deep below the surface of an alien planet only minutes before its destruction.

I had always expected, from my extensive readings of the penny dreadfuls and popular romances, that at this point the beautiful heroine would be expecting her dashing beau to come racing to her rescue to save her from a dastardly death. I can only presume I had not made sufficient effort to ensure my looks would warrant such assistance as my beau seemed to be ignoring me completely and was instead quietly and rather unhurriedly studying the buttons and lights on the consoles.

This was punctuated every few minutes by the sudden

flashing of lights and small judders of the ship assisted by his addressing the machine with explosive comments regarding its inability to do what it was told. It reminded me of a master trying to train a new puppy.

This carried on for some time during which I found it quite difficult to keep my thoughts to myself and not encourage him to do something. Eventually and thankfully he said. "OK, now we know how this spaceship works. Let's try some tests."

I was then introduced to the wonders of spaceship navigation which involved a number of involuntary and rather shaky trips around and up and down the cavern. I was reminded of a holiday by train to the Norfolk Broads where my father had hired what I believe he called a 'Gaff Sloop' or what I still refer to as a rickety, leaking, cold, wooden tub with two wet canvas sails. Oh, and I had almost forgotten the four berths covered with bedding which I can only presume the local poor house had found no longer suitable for its inhabitants. The first hour or so were spent learning the 'ropes' under our father's supervision. We were helped and encouraged by a group of locals who had gathered on the bank and who, judging by their growing numbers, had invited their acquaintances from far and wide to assist in our education. After another hour of little progress Father suggested rather unfairly that he now understood why women were not normally allowed in the Navy and perhaps we should all pack our bags and go home. However, just as we all agreed this would be a good idea, we found ourselves sailing or more accurately blown on to the Broads.

We looked back at the receding crowd on the bank who were now waving and pointing at a rope trailing in the water from the wharf. As we drifted off, we discovered, through not a little interrogation from our father which included comments on the disadvantages of raising children, that Flory, being only fourteen at the time and therefore somewhat bored, had succeeded in untying a round turn and two half hitches and detaching it from the boat. There then followed a rather unpleasant afternoon 'bumping' into bridges and banks and shouting 'Give way to Sail!' accompanied by Flory crying, at the first sign of a motor launch coming in our direction. We were eventually rescued by a rather nice and courteous man in a launch who suggested, and we agreed that it was best for everyone if we stayed in the local hostelry overnight. During dinner that evening the man appeared again and after enquiring about our welfare asked if Flory and I would like him to teach us the 'ropes' instead the next day. Unfortunately, our father must have noticed our gushing enthusiasm for this offer and using the excuse that we were still of an impressionable age decided that we must return home at the earliest opportunity for our own protection. It was only later that we discovered that our father's nautical knowledge was limited to a day's dinghy sailing with his friends on the Thames following an exceedingly late evening at their Club. And to think he was the man from whom I had sought advice for all things important in my life!

But back to this sailing ship which thankfully I noticed did not have a tethering rope. Although the controls were different from a carriage, I quickly recognised it was like a new horse. One must be responsive to its needs and limitations. It could not be persuaded beyond its capabilities. This was not the attitude of James who seemed to be doing his best to flog it to death and encouraged me to do the same. However, apart from a particularly hair-raising manoeuvre in which I had flipped it upside down and turned it into a spin he remarked that perhaps my more cautious approach had some merit.

Eventually we agreed, after taking it in turns to drive a number of times, that no further improvement in our skills could be acquired without the assistance of someone with experience or sense and that we were only in one piece because thankfully the ship could detect an imminent contact with the walls and stop just in time by itself.

There was however, one important question.

"So, James, who is going to be the driver?"

"After that amazing loop-the-loop I think you should be."

"If only I could remember how I performed that trick. But it was fun and I would like to have a go."

"Good. Then you're on. I don't think we have to worry too much because it seems to be able to know when we're doing something really stupid. Not of course that I would expect you to do such a thing."

I had not expected James to acquiesce so easily as normally he enjoyed driving anything with an engine. Sensing he may have still been trying to make amends for his Martian disappearing trick I tried to reassure him, "James?"

"Yes?"

"Despite my often rather hasty admonishments of your unexpected actions you must not conclude that I think you have a monopoly in that area. I am well aware of my own mistakes and how by chance we survived them as they often revisit me at night with a shudder. So please promise, if you feel I have reached my limits, you will take over, won't you?"

"Yes, of course I will. And vice versa."

I had sensed correctly for I could see he was relieved by

my offer.

"So we are ready." I said. "But there are still two unanswered questions. How can we move when everything else is frozen in time and more importantly, what are we supposed to do now?"

As if to answer the second, all the lights came on and the ship began to slowly move up the cavern on its own accord.

I exclaimed, "James! If in future, you even detect that I am about to make another suggestion about any subject will you please immediately bind and gag me and lock me in a darkened room where I will promise to be of no further trouble."

"I had no idea you were into that sort of thing, Elizabeth. Unfortunately, not being brought up as a Victorian gentleman, I prefer you loose and fancy free. But be assured If the occasion arises, I expect you will find me already in there to keep you company."

And with those confusing thoughts in mind I watched the spaceship continue to slowly rise towards the mouth of the cavern above.

--- ∼ ---

Chapter Eleven

J.

As we slowly ascended the cavern my first thought was why were we moving while everything else was frozen in time? And also, why was it not completely black because I reasoned if time had stopped so had all the photons. And then it occurred to me that it was only when we moved, we saw light as we interacted with it.

We eventually came to the surface and stopped. The great Tharsis Volcanoes stood silently on the plain and up above us hung the third moon, behind which was Halley's comet dangerously close.

Dangerously close! That meant...I suddenly realised we were witnessing the event before the time fracture! Elizabeth had recognised it as well.

"We have travelled through the barrier! How did we do that?"

"It must be as Wells said. We are the only ones who are able to move through time freely."

"But how do we do it? Do we think it and it just happens?"

"If that was the case, when we were first going out I would have been around to your bedroom every night."

"Do you have any thoughts in your heads that do not involve visiting respectable ladies in their bedrooms and ravishing them?"

"Nope. By the way who mentioned ravishing them?"

A slight pause. Then she said, "I think we better return to the subject in hand before I am compromised."

I said, "Good idea. Well, I think it is now up to us to do

something. Any ideas?"

"You are still asking me for suggestions, James?"

"Yes, I have faith in you."

"Very well. We find ourselves here at the beginning of time and sent by the Martians. So, I would conclude that we must do something that they want."

"Such as something which ensures that they take over our world."

"Oh, James, you are such a cynic."

"You mean a realist."

"Possibly but I am too exhausted to save the world again. Surely as they have not harmed us they would not want to do that?"

"God knows. But maybe as we seem to be the only people who can go through time unaided perhaps they are using us."

"You know you may have reason but I have just had a thought. The Martians up to this catastrophe were possibly quite happy with their world. Perhaps they want us to try and advert it."

"You mean if their planet wasn't ruined they wouldn't need our planet."

"Yes. And there in front of us is the cause of their problem, Halley's Comet."

"So you think if it could be diverted from its path a little it would avoid the third moon and prevent the disaster on Mars?"

"It would be worth a try, James."

Were Victorians really like this? Without fear? How cocooned western society had become. If I ever get back home and am accused of cowardice, I will reply that I am almost as brave as my wife.

"Ok, let's do it!" I said resignedly. "After all, we're stuck in these seats with the doors locked."

However, for some reason, possibly only known to the Martians, my suggestion was not taken up by the spaceship. It just hovered there about half a mile above the surface.

"Despite what I said earlier, James, shall I suggest it?"

"Go on then. I'll see you in the darkened room."

Nothing happened.

"It looks like we'll have to do it ourselves." I said. "Ready to be the first Victorian space pilot?"

--- ∼ ---

E.

If my friends from Girton could see me now steering a great blue ship in space, what would they think? I would love to return to one of those smoke-filled, male, monocled parties to which we ladies were invited and put on show to absorb their condescending wit. Imagine arriving dressed in jeans, a loose unbuttoned shirt and one of my bras which James found favourable and recount wondrous tales of travels in time and space. I shared this thought with James.

"That would be a sight for sore eyes, and I promise I would visit you in Bedlam afterwards as often as possible. Now let's see if we can get close to the comet."

I navigated the ship up into the sky. I found the controls surprisingly responsive and forgiving as though the ship was helping me. As we rose above the volcanoes the third moon appeared over the horizon.

As we approached the comet we began to encounter what I can only describe as white flakes of snow which became thicker until I felt we were in a windless blizzard. I could see now the comet was not solid. It was like a gigantic ball of slush from which long beams of icy vapour and dust stretched towards the Sun.

Another few minutes passed, if time was indeed the measure of our journey, and the comet had become a mass of grey and white rocky substance. It must have been five or six miles in diameter.

I decided to stop the ship.

"What shall we do?" I said.

"We drive into it and try and divert it from that moon. I think it's only slush and space dirt."

It seemed a very boyish plan.

"Is that our plan, James? Have you not heard of Lord Cardigan's disastrous adventure?"

"Yes. But those were cannon balls. I'm sure these are made of snow."

We started forward again. The ship's nose pushed into the icy surface. Great chunks broke away. It really was like a dirty snowball. For what seemed a mile we ploughed through the slush and ice.

"It's so light I think we're going to fly straight through it." I said.

And then we came to a halt.

"I think we have stopped, James."

"As in the words: try as you might it won't go any farther?"

"Yes."

"Have you tried reversing or your flip and roll?"

"Yes."

I have often thought if I was faced with imminent danger or death what I would do. Would I scream or accept my fate in stoical silence? Now faced with such a situation I discovered to my surprise that my natural response was extreme anger at everything, including the Martians, Mr Wells and myself. A few arrows even went James' way. This had no effect on him however because he was too busy being affected in the same way.

After a few minutes in which I was for once grateful James had extended my vocabulary sufficiently to express my emotions properly we calmed down.

"Well, Elizabeth, although that didn't help one jot, it was quite therapeutic. It was also a great insight into the female brain on how parts of the anatomy should be applied in situations like this."

"I prefer it if you don't mention my outburst to anyone in future or come to think of it, the past."

"Not a word. But did you really get all those words off me?"

I gave him a demurely innocent smile. "Of course, James. I hope you are not implying that before I met you I was ever in company where I might have heard such language."

"Of course not. How rude of me to even suggest it."

$$--- \sim ---$$

J.

I've never quite understood when we have been faced with almost certain death how we end up in this banter. But to quote Elizabeth's words, it is a comfort.

And that was the last 'comfort' we had for a while because the block of ice we found ourselves wedged in began to crack. Great fissures appeared running in all directions and getting wider and wider until our ice cage broke in two revealing patches of the black sky. I selected one and said,

"See that black hole there? I'm going for it!"

I took over the controls and went for it full power though I confess with my eyes shut. When I opened them again, to my surprise we were in free space and saw that the round ball of Halley's comet was now breaking up.

As the third moon crossed the sky towards the Martian horizon one chunk of the comet about twice its size caught up with it and hit it full on. The chunk must have been going far faster than moon but instead of bouncing off like a billiard ball as I expected the icy block absorbed the moon completely. It then to my amazement carried the moon off into space like a bird of prey catching a mouse.

We just looked at each other, then at the screen and then at each other again.

I let Elizabeth guide us back to the Tharsis Plain while I tried to find the hole we had come out of. There were quite a number of these round holes and luckily, we only had to go down four before we found the right one.

As we lay still, wrapped in our crash beds, Elizabeth said, "I am astounded, James, at your plan. To calculate the forces involved and trajectories all in your head and execute it with such precision. I had not realised you were capable of such a thing."

"I must admit I do surprise myself sometimes with my mental agility."

"Me too. Especially solving an N-body problem which I had understood to be unsolvable without a large computational machine."

"I know. It shows you how lucky you are going out with me."

"It is a wonder I admit and I am surprised how often I

find cause to be reminded."

Someone was getting a bit too cheeky now. I found the fasteners to the crash bed, got off and went over to Elizabeth who was still struggling with the webbing and said, "Oh dear. You seemed to be all trussed up and completely unable to move."

"James! Let me out of here." She exclaimed looking at me wondering what I was going to do.

"You have to give me a kiss first."

"Well, I suppose you deserve just one." And she screwed up her face and pouted her lips like a child having to kiss her granny.

I kissed her gently until her lips softened then pressed the release button.

"There you are. That was easy, wasn't it?"

She then got up, grabbed me and just about pushed her tongue down my throat with her passion.

"Gosh, I needed that," she said breathlessly, releasing me. "Now how do we get home?"

I must find out where women keep their on/off button. It's a hopeless task, of course, because as soon as they suspect you've found it they hide it in another secret place.

I said, "I suppose it's the time machine again though I wish I could take that ship. It would look nice parked at the front of our home in front of the neighbours. We could take trips to space whenever we want."

"I think we should stay with one adventure at a time. But I do agree it would be a talking point."

So, we reluctantly left the ship and walked over to the machine. As expected, or hoped, the door opened for us. Inside the stone Martian was still sitting on the globe.

--- ~ ---

E.

We had crossed the time barrier and possibly saved Mars although whether the Earth was saved we did not know. The display on the console said 536 AD.

I said, "I presume we are still on the other side of the time fissure."

"There's only way to find out."

James moved the time pointer forward. The screen lit up and revealed an earthly landscape with my home standing alone in front of us.. The comet could be seen on the horizon. As we moved forward it came closer and bigger. It did not look like it was going to miss. A few more days sped past and it had broken into three. One began to descend to Earth. As it hit the atmosphere it ignited into a fire ball. Hundreds of fireworks broke off it. The horizon lit red. Then the wind again. The forest around us swayed until, overcome, it blew down. Trees and vegetation flew past us. On and on it went for days. After a week there was calm, but the landscape was desolate.

James said. "It looks we may have saved Mars, but we haven't saved Earth from the Dark Ages."

I agreed but said, "It could have been much worse. Our deflection could have caused a direct hit."

We sat there contemplating the landscape. The Martian had not moved.

"Do you mind if I just test we can go back into the past? Perhaps we can see when your house was built."

I could not resist this and agreed even though I was yearning to go home.

Back we went. The fire balls receded up into space and the comet disappeared. The landscape was restored. About 450AD the forest slowly grew smaller until it became farm land. Fields of wheat and barley stretched into the South Downs which were bare of woodland and covered with the white specks of flocks of sheep.

By 400 AD derelict stone buildings appeared in the distance. Around 380 AD a large Roman red pantile roofed building repaired itself and grew in size not five hundred yards from my house. A road appeared from it which came to my home Then in 358 AD my house became a building site.

"Stop, James. I want to see it."

"Are you sure?"

"Yes. I must see how it began."

We halted and James said, "OK. Let's get out. By the way how's your Latin? 'Cos you're going to need it judging by the shape of that farmhouse over there."

___ ～ ___

J.

We stood on the grass opposite the house. For some reason when travelling in time we didn't see people. Now we could see about twenty-odd workmen busily constructing the stonework of Elizabeth 's house supervised by what I thought was a woman but turned out to be man in a toga. He also seemed to be carrying a roman sword.

While wondering what to do he spotted us and started in our direction. Not having a sword, I felt a bit vulnerable. Not that it would have made any difference. Mainly because in a previous life I had challenged a girl who did fencing to a fight. We had drunk quite a lot and were making spaghetti bolognese for about five of us. It is the meal of choice for single people. She suggested that we use spaghetti strands as swords. Perfect. "En garde!" I said. And within two seconds I was disarmed. Four spaghetti swords later I decided that the amount of beer I'd consumed was giving her an advantage. Two days later I was sober and dressed up in fencing gear for a return match. She had dyed the blocks on the end of the rapiers to aid counting the number of hits. After about ten minutes when I looked like I had a sever attack of chicken pox I conceded that some skill was involved, and men didn't genetically have superiority in fighting.

In desperation I asked Elizabeth if she had done any sword fighting but apparently it hadn't been part of her curriculum to catch a man although she thought there were occasions it would have been useful to get rid of one.

The Roman arrived. He was actually wearing the clothes you see in museums complete with a grey tunic which stopped just above his knees and cross-gartered sandals. I could tell he was a bit a confused and nervous, judging by the way he was holding the pommel of his sword, but I wasn't quite sure whether it was the time machine behind us or our attire.

Ignoring Elizabeth, he addressed me with what I presumed was Latin though it sounded Italian. I looked at Elizabeth for help and to my surprise she answered. She wasn't happy with the answer though.

"What did you say?"

"I explained you are a free man returning to Chichester with his wife."

"Well done. What did he say?"

"He asked why you keep a whore who speaks such poor Latin."

"Well, I'm shocked."

"Thank you, James. It is a small comfort."

"No, I mean, fancy you knowing the Latin word for 'whore'."

Before she could reply I said, "Tell him I don't keep my whore for her Latin."

"I will not. That would imply that my sole purpose is to be your strumpet."

I let that nice thought go and said. "Rubbish, you're quite a good cook as well. Ouch! Sorry. Try it anyway. Remember, we're in the classical world where women are regarded as only half sentient. That's why the classics were so popular at all your posh boys' schools."

"I am not going to agree that I am your, er, well, you know, just for the sake of convention. I don't want to find Elizabeth the Scortum of Noviomagus Reginorum is famous when I return home."

"Otherwise I'll be looking for my scrotum, I presume." Well, I thought it was funny.

Anyway, on hearing her reply, he laughed and gave me a good thump on the shoulder. Which was a bit weird because he was only about five foot six tall.

"Why is he laughing?"

"I told him I was your wife not your strumpet to which he replied that only a whore would marry a barbarian free man. There was then a little heated discussion about my honour during which he said that by the way I addressed him you obviously did not beat me enough! When I objected he said it proved his point and started laughing. Well, really!"

I tried to keep a very straight and concerned face.

"Seeing he could get no further sport with me, he then asked your name and when I told him he looked surprised as said it sounded Roman. Then he said to follow him."

I looked at the Roman who was beckoning me to the building. I followed him with my strumpet following dutifully behind.

--- ~ ---

E.

I wished I had paid more attention to my Latin classes although I have feeling the subject of how a respectable lady should defend herself in the unlikely situation where she was accused by a Roman officer of being a barbarian's whore was not on the curriculum. Luckily the unmannered ape whom I have often chided humorously on his lack of classical languages did not realise how useless I was in this area.

When we arrived at my house, or should I say the uncompleted shell of my house, the workmen downed tools and moved away. The Roman then took us to the newly formed entrance. James asked me to find out why they were building it.

I was not too happy about another conversation in which my marital status would be questioned and I said rather pointedly, "Do you not think he will wonder why your whore is asking all the questions?"

"Not at all. It will remind him how dutiful you are and for me to go easy on the beatings."

I must apologise to any ladies reading this but try as I might I could not gain an advantage expected of my sex in any direction. I can only presume my wit had been weakened by our adventure. I prayed I would not be stuck in this world for much longer.

After a few minutes' discussion in which I followed James' advice and assumed the role I was expected the Roman told us they were building a church over an ancient pagan place in the hope of preventing the small devils which appeared on a full moon from escaping. I thought my Latin was improving for the Roman had become quite friendly towards me though I noticed my breasts were receiving quite a lot of attention. However, I completely misinterpreted his intentions for he then had the audacity to ask James if he would sell me as he thought he could get a good price at the market as I had remarkable teeth for someone my age! As an incentive he also offered to split the difference with James!

When James asked how much, I decided that the line I had drawn for him had been crossed by some miles and female retribution must come swiftly. Though how and in what form was not immediately apparent.

However, there were more pressing needs for I noticed the doorway framed a wooden door. The same wooden door in my house in the future. James noticed too and said we should try to get in.

Before they came to an agreement on a price and sent me off to a brothel or worse I realised there was no point in trying to pretend I was not what the Roman thought and told him that my 'master' wished to enter the building.

He looked at me and then James with some horror and told me to tell my whore-keeper, as he put it, that legends recorded that no one who entered had ever come out. When I told James this, and also what his new job was, to my astonishment he went up to the door and banged on it three times.

We then stood there for over a minute feeling rather stupid while the workers and builders gathered around us nervously waiting to see what was going to happen. James was just about to have another attempt when the door opened to reveal a blank grey wall through which my father's head and hand appeared. I turned to find that James and I were alone and the other twenty-one people were running as fast as they could, screaming, towards the woods at the edge of the field.

--- ∼ ---

Chapter Twelve

J.

We were back in the drawing room. Wells, Hyatt and Elizabeth's father were sitting in their favourite chairs and Marco was enjoying a glass of wine by the fire. The Martian had disappeared. I was under pain of death not to discuss Elizabeth's new found status in the sixth century. Having not eaten for some time I demanded that they feed us before we recounted our story. To which Marco said, "Help yourself." Thanks a lot.

Elizabeth and I went into the parlour, made sure there was enough wood in the stove and I proceeded to make some cheese on toast because that's all I could find. I noticed Elizabeth was a little quieter than normal and made the mistake of asking if she was OK.

"Oh, thank you, Sir, for enquiring after my health. I had not expected your strumpet to be treated with such concern."

I just managed to stop myself from replying with similar banter and said. "Look, I'm sorry but my main concern was to keep that Roman's sword in its sheath and a smile on his face. As far as I can tell from the history books they're all psychopaths, you know. I was scared witless! He could have grabbed you and carried you off and finished me with a single thrust."

"A gentleman in my time would have made some effort to defend my honour!" She shot back while looking away from me at the wall.

"Yes, and he would have been chopped up into dog meat.

Can you imagine your cousin Henry defending you? They'd have had his head on a spike in a thrice."

She looked down at her shoes then back at me. "I admit you have reason. But would you have let him carry me off?"

"What do you think?" I could see she wanted a plain answer. "OK. You know I would have fought. But the end result would have been the same."

"I know, James. It is such a different world."

"Right, burnt toast and cheese is ready and tea's on the way. I bet you wouldn't get many husbands doing this in your time."

"No. They would be too busy defending their wives' honour."

I let her have the last word and we sat down to eat our food. We were very tired.

---~---

E.

Sometimes re-establishing equality in a marriage is, in hindsight, not as pleasurable as one hopes. Emotion and practicality get so entangled.

After the plate of cheese on toast and tinned pineapples in syrup we returned to the drawing room where we recounted our tale, leaving out my new-found profession.

However, it was nearly revealed when my good father enquired how I had fared, dressed as I was, in the world out there. Luckily, we avoided the subject though James later remarked my nails were rather sharp and had almost drawn blood from his arm.

Mr Wells tried to summarise, "It seems you have managed to cross the time fracture, damaged the comet so that a piece broke away and expertly hit the third moon carrying it off into space."

Mr Batalia thought he would interject with a little of his sardonic wit. "Very impressed, Urquhart, managing to do that. Sure it wasn't just a lucky accident?"

James replied, "Believe what you like. It saved Mars."

"Yes, but you didn't save the Dark Ages, did you?"

"Oh, I'm sorry, Marco. If only you had volunteered to come with us it would have made all the difference." replied James with as much controlled venom as he could muster.

Mr Wells thankfully deflected them. "You may have noticed our little friend has disappeared. I believe it has returned to Mars. If what you say is true and Mars has avoided a major catastrophe, it will be wanting to see its world again."

James who was now looking decidedly exhausted, remarked, "Yes, I would like to see what the colour of Mars is in the sky now. But could we discuss this another time? We would like to go home to a comfy bed and sleep for about three days."

"Of course." said Mr Wells. Iit would be a good time to go now anyway as we are running out of food and the first waves of Saxons are coming."

"So how do we do it?"

"You'll need the time machine."

James expressed my thoughts. "What? We're not going out there again! I'll be chopped up and my wife will be sold off to market."

"Why would you think that?" said Mr Batalia, astutely cornering us.

"Only from what I've read about the Roman Empire," replied James weakly, caught on the hoof but with just enough conviction.

"Nevertheless," said Wells, interrupting, "I'm afraid it's the only way out unless you want to stay in this house forever in 1895."

"Have you not visited the outside since you came here?" I said with some astonishment.

"Yes, but each time you arrived the world out there changed to the time you were in."

"How does that happen?" said James.

Mr Wells thought for a moment, "It is a quandary. We can only conclude that you two must have special powers which we don't understand."

James said, "I don't believe I'm anything special. Though obviously Elizabeth is, but it's more likely it comes from the time machine out there."

"What can that do?" said Marco. "Remember, I put that together."

"That could explain a lot." said James, about to start another round of verbal fisticuffs. However, I could see what James was thinking.

"Maybe the space-time field generated by the machine leaks into the surrounding area and is picked up by any portals that may be in the vicinity."

I do wish sometimes that when I speak about anything other than what women are expected to say the company of men in my presence would not look so surprised.

"That would make some sense," said James. "And any portals, like that door for instance, flips into that time state until, to paraphrase Newton, an external force acts on it to change its state. What do you think, Marco? Does your machine leak?"

"I've no idea. I never saw any effects but then I've always

been inside the machine when it's started up. Mind you, it's got a Martian power source. God knows what that's doing to all the dimensions."

James continued to goad Mr Baralia. "Ever thought of doing a risk assessment before you start playing about with the universe, Marco? You're not thinking about making a black hole by any chance?"

"What do you think powers time?"

"What do you mean? Time ends or stops at the event horizon of the black hole."

"Or that's where it starts, Urquhart. Does time run backwards or forwards?"

"Ah," sighed James. " The old entropy question. Third law of thermodynamics. Time only travels one way. In the direction from order to disorder."

"Wrong time, Urquhart. I'm talking about time, the fourth dimension. The one that all things travel on from the past to the future. You've seen it, haven't you? The Martians have shown you?"

He was right. I recalled seeing the planets as the Martians did, extruding into twisting corkscrew paths around the Sun. In my mind I felt I could have reached down and touched any point in their past or future. As I imagined it again I suddenly realised what we did when we travelled. I said, "So to reach the past or future we have to travel out of time."

"Exactly, Mrs Urquhart. Once again you've hit the nail on the head."

"And to do that," said James, "you need a fifth dimension to travel in."

"Well done, Urquhart. You're catching up with your wife again."

"I'll let her be the judge of that." replied James thankfully ignoring the jibe. "Anyway, my brain's full. So how are you lot getting back?"

I'd forgotten about my father.

"We have to come with you." said Mr Wells.

So all six of us packed our bags and I changed into my green Victorian garments as I could not cope with any more comments on my dress or position in life.

James was the first to look through the door. "OK, it's dark out there and I can't see anyone but that could mean they're all waiting to trap the first devil that comes out of this building. I think it's best if I go out first and scout around unless you want to do it, Marco. It must be your turn by now."

Mr Batalia looked at us all. There was a glint of something in his eye. Then he shrugged his shoulders and said. "Very well. I'll go first." I realised what he was thinking and stopped him. "No, you are not. You would take the machine without us."

He tried to deny it but I could see I had hit the mark.

"Any other volunteers? OK. It's me then" said James resignedly, then looking at me a little dejectedly, "I have to prove a point to someone anyway."

I hope I do not push James too hard. This equality of the sexes in his world is a delight. But I sometimes wonder whether being released from my world where the position of the woman is generally confined to the parlour and the nursery I take too much advantage. I have mentioned this to him once or twice to which he has replied in his usual diplomatic fashion that 'it keeps him on his toes'. What a difference to the treatment of women in the Roman world.

However, I could not let him go out there by himself for I always have this fear that if we are separated we will lose each other in time. There was also, I thought rather selfishly, that the probability of ending up in the market might be reduced if I had four gentleman defending me. Though when I looked at them in their variety of fashions, I didn't give much hope.

Nevertheless, I said forcefully. "No! We all go as one." Everyone agreed, with the exception of Mr Batalia and gathering our luggage, a motley crew of strangely dressed devils one by one materialised out through the door.

$$--- \sim ---$$

J.

A gibbous moon was rising in the east silhouetting the tree line. It was just as we approached the machine, I noticed them all in a row by the side of the house. We stopped in our tracks and moved much closer to each other. Though what protection that gave us I've no idea. It looked like half the villa estate had turned up complete with the Roman with the toga and sword. Next to him I could see a woman and what looked like a child. When they saw us they immediately fell to the ground in some sort of obeisant position of reverence.

Both groups lay or stood motionless not daring to move until Elizabeth, who has no fear, decided to take control after some mutterings about men and how you can't depend on them when you need them.

She called to the Roman in her latin to stand up and bring his family with him. To my surprise his wife stood up first! I have to admit his wife was quite a beauty and had gone to some lengths to put on her Sunday best. Her dress, which seemed to be embroidered in silk fairy flowers, I would have bought Elizabeth without asking the price. It was only partially covered, as only women can partially cover themselves to reveal all, by that white loosely hanging smock which signified her marital status and held by two intricate gilt shoulder straps. Her hair must have been very long for it was plaited high up in many intricate knots and in the moonlight her face was pure white. She then spoke to her husband which by its delivery did not need translation and caused him to stand up as well. Having got him to his feet she then approached us and with some confidence which suggested she had concluded we weren't Gods from Heaven, she addressed Elizabeth directly. Why she thought Elizabeth was in charge of five men I've no idea. Anyway, there then followed a rather fast Latin conversation accompanied by much pointing at their respective husbands. Apparently, according to my nearest and dearest, who I believe absolutely at all times, the Roman's wife apologised for her husband questioning her status but added if I, that is the large barbarian next to her, had shown a bit more defence of Elizabeth's honour some of the comments by her husband would not have been made! How two women can take control over six men I don't know.

The Roman's wife then said, glancing at her husband who was studiously staring at his feet for much of the conversation and looked like he would welcome an offer to go down the pub with me for a beer, that to make amends they had built a shrine in our honour in the porch of the house and carved our family name Urquhart beneath it. She then took us over to the door where there was now a carved oval recess below which cut in the stone block were the letters VQVT. I now understood where that worn recess with what looked like our name came from. However, within this alcove they had placed a small stone figure which looked like a hare. There was something a wrong with it though. I thought perhaps they had been in a hurry to finish it. Then I looked closer and realised what was wrong. It wasn't a hare; it was the spitting image of a Martian!

I asked Elizabeth to ask them what it was to which they replied by pointing to the sky or more exactly to Mars which had now appeared between the clouds. To my surprise it was still orange. I wanted to ask more, but everyone else just wanted to get to the time machine while we were all in one piece.

However, I was quite touched by what they had done for us considering if I had been one of them and met us in the way they had I would still be running towards Rome and I thought something in return was required before we left. A gift from the gods perhaps; I beckoned the husband to me. He looked askance at his wife who nodded. I smiled at him and shrugged my shoulders to signify I was also in the doghouse and no more in control than he was. He returned the same gestures in recognition. I then took off my solar-powered luminous watch and asked for his hand. It was a hand that had seen hard work although whether it was soldering, farming or both I didn't know. I slid it onto his wrist and showed him how to close the titanium clasp. He immediately recognised what it did and showed his daughter and wife whose eyes lit up like his in wonder.

Elizabeth said. "That was very nice of you. I know that is almost as precious as your phone. I must follow your example and give something as well. Do you think some knowledge of our world would be nice?"

"I'm not sure. Remember the Prime Directive."

"What is that?"

"Star Trek? Captain Kirk? No? Well, basically it means don't help the butterfly out of the chrysalis no matter how hard it struggles."

"Ah, I see. One must find one's own way in the world. And I thought you were a socialist, James." she teased.

"I am," I replied. " I make the garden, plant the flowers and show the birds and bees what to do. But after that it's up to them."

She produced a pocketbook and pencil and took it to the child who at first immediately clutched her mother. She opened the note book and proceeded in the dim moonlight to draw a teddy bear and a cat. She asked the child's name which was Aurelia, and wrote it on the page. Then after pointing at us she wrote our names underneath and the date 350 AD followed by 'CCCL Anno Domini'. Elizabeth then gave the girl the pocketbook and pencil.

"Do you think that would change their civilisation?"

Aurelia was already busy scribbling in the notebook assisted by her mother.

I said, "Compared with seeing us come out that door and then in a minute disappear in the time machine, I don't think so."

 I was dying to point out to her that the AD system wasn't invented until at least the sixth century.   But then decided best to bank it ready for the next time Elizabeth pointed out on of my minor errors.

I shook hands with my fellow sufferer and asked Elizabeth to tell him if he ever fancied a beer to give me a call.

--- ∼ ---

E.

We entered the machine. It was a little crowded and I have to admit after a few minutes I would have welcomed the opening of a window to allow in some fresh air.

James went over to the controls and asked when people wanted to go. He was, like me, exhausted. Mr Wells and Mr Hyatt wished to be 'dropped off' in 1895. Oh, to be home! My father wanted to return to 1873 where he started.

Which left Mr Batalia.

I thought of leaving him here with the Romans but reluctantly admitted to myself that would bring me down to his level. James suggested the Moon might be appropriate. We eventually decided that James' period would be acceptable where we could keep an eye on him. After some hesitation during which James offered a number of other life-shortening locations he agreed. Which was a little disconcerting because I knew he was a slippery fish.

As we went forward in time we saw once again the spectacle of the comet and the end of Roman civilisation. Then on we went, watching my house rebuild itself.

Firstly, we dropped off Mr Batalia in 2016. James thought he could do with a walk so let him out in a field near Winchester. We departed before he knew where he was. Then we said our goodbyes to Mr Wells and My Hyatt. I said. "Please do not construe this the wrong way, Mr Wells, but I hope we don't meet again for a while."

He gave an enigmatic smile and quipped, "There is time enough for everyone, Mrs Urquhart."

We then returned to our Hamgreen in 1873, closed down the machine, stepped out in to the courtyard and inhaled the fresh autumn evening air. James immediately went over to the pillar by the doorway. The worn alcove was still there and I could see now the worn lines of our name. However, I had not expected to see the little stone Martian sitting in the recess as fresh and as new as when we saw it last.

I pulled the bell cord and in a moment, Flory answered the door. There was no portal. This was followed by a very affectionate welcome from my sister for our father.

___~___

J.

I must have lain in the bath for a good half hour. I had suggested to Elizabeth that to save on hot water we could share it but she felt that there was not room enough for two and in any case it would be unfair for me to have the tap end. She also said the maid servant was unavailable to scrub my back and if I asked again she would send Henry up with a wire brush.

We were then treated to an excellent Victorian dinner. Elizabeth and Flory had dressed in ballroom finery and I was wearing a Victorian dinner suit which she said would considerably reduce the opportunities for remarks on gardening. As far as I can remember there were one hundred and twenty courses if you didn't include the side plates of ham, veal and mutton on the sideboard and I can only presume its preparation had laid waste the surrounding ten miles of countryside, judging by the number of birds, fowl and small animals served in the French fashion of 'if it's alive you can eat it'.. Beside my plates were five coloured glasses which I discovered were all for me. These were expertly filled by a servant with champagne, hock, madeira, red wine and port.

I say expertly for I never saw him fill or refill them, yet for some reason they were always full. It was like drinking from a cornucopia. Try as I might I could not empty a glass. It was only later I discovered that he had the dastardly trick of only filling my glasses when I was distracted by conversation.

Eventually the eating and drinking stopped, mainly on their discovery that I was actually full to the point of bursting but had thought it impolite to leave the table without finishing everything.

We men then retired, or staggered, to the smoking room. Apparently in this house someone else did the washing up. I declined the offer of a smoke but within ten minutes the small room was so filled with cigar fumes from her father and Henry that I felt as if I had smoked a couple anyway.

After a while and a whiskey or two I asked if we could get out of the fug and go and look at the stars from the conservatory.

It was a cool clear frost-bright night and the stars twinkled brightly in the haze of the alcohol. Two planets lay just between Orion and Taurus. One was distinctly orange. The telescope was still sitting in the corner so I asked if I could use it. After a few seconds of trying to focus, which I found easier once I had removed the end cap, I found Jupiter with two of its Galilean moons. I then turned to the other planet. It was Mars. The north and south poles were now blue white like the colour of an iceberg. Over much of the surface there was orange desert but here and there were large patches of green connected by lines. I put a higher magnification lens in and after more fiddling with the-focus I saw at last the canals of Mars. They were ice blue. I wondered how the Martians were getting on and whether they knew we had saved their world.

___ ~ ___

E.

The men eventually returned to the drawing room to join Flory and I. During their absence I had extracted enough information about Henry and her by posing enough disinterested enquiries and oblique references to keep Jill and I amused for a whole evening. Once the men were seated, and Henry had managed to fit his plain-glass monocle into his eye-socket without it falling out, ((one of the sillier of the male fashions of the time) we offered them some savouries, but James declined saying that he had excelled himself even by his standards at dinner. I must admit I agreed and pointing at our ancestors on the wall reminded him if he continued with his regime he would look like them in no time at all.

About one o'clock James suggested we should go home to our time. However, I was enjoying the comfort of my old home and family asked if he minded if we stayed here a few days with my father. He looked a little disappointed and seemed to indicate by his expression and manner which I hope was not noticed by anyone else that he would prefer the company of my body rather than my home. There was no need for signals from him as I had presumed the 'sleeping' arrangements were already 'a given', as he would say. However, he agreed to stay. As it was now getting late everyone decided it was time to retire. I went upstairs first where I was met by my maid Lilly.

"I have put Mr Urquhart in the guest bedroom. I hope that is convenient, Miss Lizzy" she said with a smile. I nearly blurted out that it was not 'convenient' when I suddenly remembered Henry's instructions and why James had made his expression in the drawing room.

I replied rather unconvincingly that it would suffice and thanked her. To which she added, with that look she reserved for me that indicated nothing ever got past her, that unfortunately the key to the door of the guest bedroom had unaccountably gone missing and could not be locked and hoped that would not cause any 'inconvenience'. Seeing by my countenance, which I tried unsuccessfully to hide, that I understood her implication she then wished me good night and walked back to her room humming a song to herself.

--- ∼ ---

Chapter Thirteen

An Interlude

E.

I awoke to a bright, warm morning. Jill had packed my beautiful silk nightdress patterned in fairy gold and azure gossamer wings and embroidered with wild flowers which James had brought me in a rather expensive shop in North Street. He said, and I agreed, that it caressed me so smoothly and softly that when he closed his eyes, he could not tell it was not my body.

We had been staying at my home at Hamgreen for almost a week now in separate chambers to comply with my cousin Henry's request. I must admit I had hoped for more intimacy but I had discovered the presence of Henry and the staff in my house caused quite some inhibitions in James' advances. He was convinced, through possibly too many reminders from myself, that my honour must be preserved at all costs. This was not helped by the servants who unbeknownst to us understood we were an item and took great delight in being in the 'wrong' place when any advance towards me was expected. My maid Lilly who had still not found the missing key was complicit in these games and having obtained from me by her usual devious questioning that James and I normally shared the same bed 'to save on heating' had wagered that I could not entice him to bed before the end of the week. As I had not had the opportunity to be with James since we left our home, and after five nights only twenty feet from his unlocked bed

151

room, I was driven to thinking a sign with the words. 'Respectable Lady requires a good ravishing by Mr. James Urquhart. Enquire within." would help. But I felt even in his times with its laissez-faire attitude to bedding this would have overstepped the mark. So, yesterday evening, the sixth evening of enforced abstinence, I paid Lilly her wager and asked for her assistance. An opportunity had arrived when Henry and Flory were invited to a soirée at Pulborough which required an overnight stay. Lilly arranged for the other staff to have a night off. She would stay to arrange breakfast but would be unaccountably missing at bedtime to assist in my undressing.

And so here I was at last with the morning sunlight peeking through the curtains. My movement woke James who had been sleeping peacefully next to me.

"What are you doing here, Elizabeth?"

I could see much to my delight that he had momentarily forgotten where he was.

"I am at a loss, James. You must have abducted me."

A flicker of panic crossed his face then he remembered. He drew me to his body and said with a smile.

"Was that shortly after you came to my room late last night and asked for assistance in undoing a stuck clasp on your evening dress."

"I cannot see how that simple request could lead to the position I find myself in here". I teased.

"Perhaps it was the discovery that you seemed to have dressed without putting on your underclothes".

"It was very warm, James. And besides if a gentleman, while helping a lady with a difficulty, noticed she had forgotten her undergarments he would immediately avert his gaze and not mention it."

"Absolutely. Except I remember that there was an extraordinary number of 'stuck" clasps which required attention, most of which I found surprisingly easy to undo."

"I must admit I was surprised by your dexterity in the dim light of the candles. It was as though you were well versed in such an occupation."

"Mmh! I think it was your direction and instruction that greatly aided the task. However, I was more surprised when on removing the last clasp the upper half of your dress inexplicably fell to your waist".

"I can only surmise I miscounted the number of fasteners, for I am sure there were more than eighteen. I would not normally allow such a thing to happen unintentionally."

"I am glad to hear it. And I hope you will forgive me for covering your breasts with my hands in case an unwanted intruder appeared at the door".

"I thank you for your concern for I would not have thought it my first reaction in such a situation. However, if such an interruption had occurred I would have listened with great interest to your explanation on how you were protecting my modesty".

"I must admit it would have taken some ingenuity to deflect such a person from drawing an erroneous conclusion."

"Quite so. But I should also remind you that kissing both of them before they were properly introduced is generally not regarded as etiquette in my time."

"I beg your pardon but I did ask each in turn and by their attitude I am sure they conveyed a certain willingness to participate."

"Then I must apologise for their manners for it seems I cannot depend on them to defend my honour in your presence when such an offer is made."

"Well, I'm sure I would have done nothing to compromise your honour and anything you remember after that would have been only a dream."

"Gosh! I am much relieved to hear that. As a maiden only slightly used I cannot imagine that I would have allowed myself to participate in the revelry that occurred last night."

In truth after his prolonged attentions to my body I had begged him like a wanton strumpet to plough me 'till the springs broke.

--- ~ ---

J.

A beam of sunlight played upon our bed through the curtain gently swaying in a summer breeze. We lay there half dozing exchanging banter when there was a knock at the door. My first thought was Henry.

A woman's voice called, "Mr Urquhart, may I come in to arrange your room?"

Without waiting for a reply, the door opened. It was Elizabeth's maid, Lilly. I just managed to push Elizabeth under the bedclothes before she entered.

"Good morning, Mr Urquhart. I hope you slept well. You don't by any chance know where my mistress is?"

I felt Elizabeth tighten her grip on my arm.

"I'm afraid I don't, Lilly."

"Oh well, I'm sure she'll turn up. Let's open the curtains and let the sun in. Oh, I see Jacob's out in the fields early and hard at work. Judging by the number of farrows you'd think he'd been ploughing all night."

I had the distinct impression a game was about to be

played at my expense.

"I'm sure he must make hay while the sun shines". I said for no other reason that it was the first farming phrase that came into my head.

I caught a glimpse of a smile as she continued to look out of the window. "Would you both like breakfast in bed or in the parlour?"

The grip tightened. It was beginning to hurt.

"I'll have breakfast downstairs though I cannot speak for Elizabeth as I don't know where she is."

"Perhaps you could ask that big fat lump under your bedding?"

A faint squeal came from under the sheets.

"Did I hear a mouse, Mr Urquhart?"

"Surely not, Lilly. It would suggest you were neglecting your cleaning duties and to answer your question, that's just a pillow to stop me falling out of bed. I hope you're not implying that as a guest here I have seduced the mistress of the house and brought her to bed?"

"I am sure that you did not do the seducing, Mr Urquhart, and it says much about you and your care for my mistress. By the way I think I see Flory coming down the road on that grey filly of hers".

Elizabeth leapt out of the bed clothes "What?"

Elizabeth and her sister Flory were great friends but as a receptacle for juicy private gossip Flory leaked like a sieve.

"Oh, good morning, Miss Lizzy. Would you like me to serve breakfast here?" said Lilly

"Certainly not! Where is Flory?"

She looked out of the window again.

"Oh, silly me. My eyesight must be failing; it was the milk maid."

"And I suppose when you return to the parlour I will be the butt of all jokes?"

"No more than usual, Miss Lizzy. Though they will be pleased to know they can stop chasing Mr Urquhart in his attempts to make advances towards you".

The reason for a number of unaccountable encounters with the servants in the orangery, the study and behind the stairs now became apparent.

I turned to Elizabeth. "Are all servants like this?"

"Certainly not! I blame you and my father for being over familiar with them."

"We are only here to serve, Miss Lizzy, " said Lilly, "Now as I've found you I will be away to make your breakfast. Oh, by the way, Miss Lizzy, I almost forgot. As it is not the end of the week here is that florin you gave me". And she left the room.

"What's the money for?" I said.

She gave a demure innocent look.

"Don't tell me you had a wager that you could seduce me before the end of the week?"

She came closer.

"Are you complaining, James?"

--- ~ ---

Chapter Fourteen

E.

Before we left my home James spent some time in our garden making copious notes on its design and contents. Our gardener, Arthur, who normally mumbles that we have no consideration for his work was much impressed by James' interest and helped him with the identification of flowers and plans for a garden. He was so impressed that as a reward he provided him with packets of dried seeds on whose covers he made James write instructions on their cultivation.

As we prepared our luggage and changed into clothing more fitting for our destination, I asked James what we should do when we returned to his time. He sighed and rubbing his stomach said he needed to 'detox' for a week with a regime devoid of pie and cream and also find a place to hide the time machine as parking it on the drive might cause some comment amongst the neighbours. I suggested we could put it in the garage after we have removed and sold the contents as on being questioned previously on their use and importance he had difficulty giving a satisfactory answer. However, this was turned down. Instead he proposed we could put it in our small garden and pretend it was an objet d'art. I thought we could pass it off as a garden shed where it would have the added advantage as a depository for the remainder of his clothes and allow me more space for my wardrobe. This caused an unprovoked stern reaction which involved a certain lady of impeccable reproach being given warning of 'a good seeing to' at the earliest opportunity.

After we had said our farewells and adieus to my family

and collected a number of boxes of seeds and plants we opened the door. James stopped and said, "I've just remembered we've got to collect the car from Midhurst! It'll be covered in parking tickets or towed away."

"Perhaps if we had a time machine we could circumvent some of the fines." I suggested.

"Gosh, if only we had one."

I agreed joining in his humour.

"No! I mean if only we had one!"

I looked into courtyard. The machine was not there. We were stranded in my time!

--- ~ ---

J.

There was only one thing left to do. Go to the cavern at Midhurst. Elizabeth and Smethers made ready the dog cart and we threw our bags in the back. Halfway down the drive I remembered what century we were in and we turned back and changed back into Victorian clothes again much to the confusion of everybody. After another half mile we returned again and collected candles and matches as I didn't want to steal them from the church a second time. You can never have enough candles.

The roads were quite muddy and rutted and Elizabeth drove while I closed my eyes. When we got on to the smoother Macadam highway, she thought she'd have some sport and said, "Would you like to hold the reins? You will find it as easy as a steering wheel. Just pull to the left or right and you will find Nelly will follow instantly."

I took the reins in my hands very carefully and before I knew it we were off. After a few seconds I thought it would be beneficial to see where we were going and to my horror saw what looked like a mail coach coming in the other direction.

"What side do I go?" I yelled as it got closer and Nelly got faster having mistaking my shout for a command to bolt.

"Why, the other side, James!"

I pulled the left rein and to my surprise veered over to the right. I pulled the other one involuntarily before I went into the ditch and immediately back to the left after another tug.

"What are you doing?" She said looking where I was going.

"I'm doing as you said!"

She looked at the reins. "Oh, you fool! You have them crossed. Give them to me." And she grabbed them out of my hands and deftly pulled Nelly and us over just in time to miss the passing coach.

When I'd recovered, I said, "How would I know they were crossed over?"

"It is a simple thing. Follow the line of a rein. Look!"

I tried again with some success though stayed as close to the centre of the road as possible much to the annoyance of other carriages. Eventually Elizabeth took pity on me, or to put it more bluntly, 'saved our lives' by taking over control again after a carriage stopped and the lady who Elizabeth knew and later categorised as part of the snooty north Chichester set enquired whether she needed assistance.

When I replied that we were alright thanks she looked at me rather haughtily then at Elizabeth and said, "Do you allow your servants to speak when they are not spoken to?"

I said in the nicest way I could. "Yes, she does obviously otherwise I wouldn't be speaking to you."

I liked the shock on her face so I thought I'd carry on. "And in case you're wondering what service I provide; I serve as her husband."

"This is your husband, Miss Bicester?" she said, still not acknowledging my existence. Her eyes were quite wide now but not as wide as her mouth which I thought I'd continue to fill. But Elizabeth got in first.

"It is Mrs Urquhart, Lady Harrington. And this is my husband, James Urquhart, otherwise known to those who know him well as Captain Adventurus, Saviour of Worlds, Traveller of Times, Occasional Defender of his Wife's Honour and Chief Wizard of the Pointy Hat Club."

I quite liked the last one. The second from last I realised I needed to work on a bit more.

Lady Whatsit looked at me again, this time with her mouth tightly shut. I said, "Yep. I know what you're thinking. I'm batting way above my class."

"I do not think judging by your attire that you know what class is."

"I find with a salary of £22,000 a year, I don't need to."

Quoting my meagre salary in the twentieth century to a Victorian had the intended effect.

"Well, really! What is the world coming to when a woman judges a man by his money rather than his class? I do not know what to think."

"I am sure you do not, Lady Harrington," said Elizabeth, "but I am sure within the next hour or so when you are with your society again you will not only know what to think but also exactly what to say. But I must bid you good day for we have a certain time to catch. I wish you a pleasant journey." And with that rather cutting reply which could be construed to offer no offence Elizabeth took the reins and off we went. I have to hand it to Elizabeth. I try to start a class war and she wins it for me without any argument for or against.

A little further down the road she said, "I do not think I will be asked to her whist parties for a while."

"Will you miss them?"

"I do not know. I've never been invited," she said with a smile.

___ ~ ___

E.

We arrived at Midhurst and reserved the White Room at the Coaching Inn for the night and asked the proprietor if he would look after Nelly and our dog cart. From not a little experience I was concerned that after we visited the cavern we may not return for some time, if time was the right word. I therefore wrote a short letter to my father informing him of the whereabouts of Nelly and having sealed it asked the proprietor if he would dispatch it to my father in the morning. If we returned beforehand, I would make an excuse and retrieve the letter.

Having gathered sufficient baggage and James' candles we walked to the cavern tunnel via the vestry in the church. Once again, we attracted notice. Twice we were stopped by passers-by and asked if we needed assistance with our luggage. Then an old lady stopped and taking pity on us, presuming that we had been evicted from our accommodation and destitute, offered James a temporary gardening job. His reply, for some reason, was not as polite as I would expect for such a generous offer. And when she left us he whispered, with some annoyance that he would promise at the first opportunity to purchase some decent

162

clothes.

The door to the cavern was still there. James pushed it open gently to find that our last hope that we might find a time machine had evaporated. But the cavern was not empty. The consoles and Earth globe were still in place. James rushed to the time dials and set them to 2016 but as I expected nothing happened for we had previously shut down the power servers. He turned to me and holding my hand said, "I'm afraid I'm going to live here with you in your time. Can you accept that?"

I replied, "Of course. We will find a way. Shall we go?"

And so we retraced our steps back along the tunnel. We passed through the vestry and into the nave thankful this time at not having to borrow any clothes to blend in. Or so we thought for as we entered the nave I realised immediately we were in a different time by the dark screens advertising church services which someone had thought if they were attached to the main pillars they would improve the religious ambience.

I asked James when he thought we were for it looked very much his world.

"I don't know. Sometime-line near mine. We have two choices. One is to go back, change our clothes again and then return to find we are in another time or just get on with it and pretend we're dressed up like this for the tourists."

We chose the latter.

--- ∼ ---

J.

As we emerged out of the church and on to the road everything not only looked familiar but was very familiar.

Gone were the silent electric cars replaced by petrol and diesel machines. Yellow lines, road signs, road works and shops selling stuff people didn't know they needed filled the street. I was home. No, I mean really home. This was the world I was in when I first met Elizabeth.

I guess she recognised it as well, judging by the way she squealed, and flung her arms around my neck before landing the loudest kiss ever on my grinning cheek.

--- ~ ---

Epilogue

E.

Our return journey was much commented upon by the surprising number of old people on the bus, many of whom examined our clothing quite closely and remarked how authentic it looked. I was also complimented on my diction by some who despaired of the youth of today and their slack language. It reminded me of my father who was a stickler for picking on any slang that was spoken in the house.

But now at last we were home. We had spent a pleasant afternoon in the autumn sunlight weeding the garden and raking leaves from the grass which we put on a small bonfire James had delighted in building.

Later as we reclined cuddled up in James' rather worn but comfy sofa with Chopin playing in the background after a surprisingly light vegetarian dinner James turned to me and said, "Would you like to go on a ramble with my friends in this wonderful countryside next Sunday?"

I could think of nothing more perfect. The leaves were still in colour and we could enjoy the last warmth of the late autumn sun.

"Oh yes, James, I would love to meet them and perhaps," I said with a smile, "there might be a cricket match at Hamgreen we could visit as well."

His face dropped. It was a picture. "No, James, I was only kidding. Wild horses could not drag me there. We will draw a big circle around it and avoid it at all costs."

But of course, when we looked for it on the map later, only for curiosity you understand, we found it was not there. For after all, James and I are only but a dream out of time.

--- ~ ---

The End

---~---

Other books by this author

from the
Time Travel Diaries of James Urquhart and Elizabeth
Bicester

Book 1 Out of Time

The first diaries of the humorous and sometimes romantic time travel adventures of James Urquhart, minor science lecturer living in 2015 and Elizabeth Bicester, lady of leisure, whom he stumbles upon at a cricket match at Hamgreen in 1873. Despite their banter regarding each other's manners they manage through incredible feats of illogical deduction and with not a little help from James Maxwell, H. G. Wells, the Martians and some strange time devices, to save the world.

Book 2 A Drift Out of Time

In this volume, they have returned home to find they are not only in an alternative future but a different aspect of themselves. To get back to their world they must travel between Mars and Earth, drifting across time and space, until eventually they reach home and discover who the Martians really are.

Book 3 A House Out of Time

Once again, the intrepid couple have "retired' to a quiet life of ease in an alternative world after helping the Martians save the Earth and their own planet. Unfortunately, Elizabeth thought it would be a good idea to visit her ancestral home at Hamgreen to see what had become of it.

….Such is the curiosity of women.

Book 4 The Space Between Time

In these extracts from the Time Travel Diaries we find the intrepid couple enjoying a peaceful and romantic picnic by the River Rother when a motor launch turns up complete with Mr Wells.

Apparently, a certain Mr Tesla has conducted one of his electro-magnetic experiments which has fractured time and dumped everyone in an alternative world of 1895. The problem is that only a few people have noticed the difference.

Mr Wells wondered if James and Elizabeth would like to help.

Book 5 The Time Palace of Mars

If you are taking your Victorian wife to a car wash for the first time, it's a good idea to explain beforehand that the long blue furry cloths banging on the windows are not aliens trying to abduct her.

This will give you more time to think of a reason why both of you are suddenly transported to a palace on Mars where Time stands still and you're surrounded by twelve strangely magical statues of mythological Gods.

Luckily Mr Puddlewick, a bank teller from Threadneedle Street is on hand to help. Even though he has no idea, after attending a lecture by Mr Tesla in New York on communicating with Mars, why he is there.

All he knows, apart from what is behind the frescos on the walls of the Palace, is that he found a strange device which had a picture of Elizabeth and I with a message "Get Urquhart". So, he pressed the Red Button.

Short Stories

The Webs of Time

\\short stories from the time travel diaries of James Urquhart, minor scientist, who lived in 2015 and Elizabeth Bicester whom he met at cricket match in 1873.

They are narrated by Professor Rolleston who discovered the original diaries and who spent his life, when not hunting fairies, trying to understand their contents and the reasons for their existence.

Three of the stories, Northern Nights, A Holiday in Cornwall and the Haunted Mill, previously appeared in Three Tales Out of Time.

About the Author

Bruce is a retired Health Physicist who lives with his wife on the south coast of England, just a few minutes' walk from the sea. When he's not researching King Arthur, he's out walking on the South Downs with his wife and his friends trying to remember all the names of the flowers and mushrooms his wife has identified.

When it's raining he can be found sometimes in his "shed" as his wife calls it, trying to master new jazz chords.

A life of writing scientific reports and reading early science fiction, especially the genre of time travel such as the works of Anderson, Simak and Wells encouraged him to start writing his own novels about the adventures of a modern man and a Victorian lady whom he met at a cricket match in 1873.

His stories have been described as "Tom Holt meets P.G. Wodehouse meets Philip K. Dick meets Fortean Times."

You can get more information on this and his other books and hobbies at: his blog at:

www.timetraveldiaries.co.uk

Or you can visit our website at:

www.aldwickpublishing.com

A House Out of Time